MOMENTUM

Montessori, a Life in Motion

MOMENTUM

Montessori, a Life in Motion

E.G. Slade

atmosphere press

For My Children

Contents

Author's Note

In my 35 years as a Montessori teacher, coach, and administrator, I have spent countless hours thinking about the Montessori philosophy. My curiosity about Maria Montessori's personal life only arose when I spent long hours away from my own young children supporting public Montessori programs in Springfield, Massachusetts. As I missed family dinners, school performances, and special outings, I thought of the sacrifices which supported the development of Montessori's work and, thus, the rise of the Montessori method.

As a woman living in Italy at the turn of the century, during a time when women were not educated past elementary school, Maria Montessori became one of the first female doctors in the country. In the midst of this, out of wedlock, she had a child. In a place steeped in Catholicism, this transgression could have ended her nascent career.

What she did, and the dilemma it reveals, captivates me. How did a woman who went on to devote her life to the development of children decide to have her only child raised by another family in the country? How did she feel about the choice?

This book is a result of those questions. It moved me to go beyond what is available in history into the waters of historical fiction. Dr. Montessori wrote a diary that chronicles her first voyage to America, *Maria*

Montessori Sails to America. That diary became the inspiration for the book you hold in your hands. Many of the sensory details and facts of the journey in *Momentum* are taken directly from her observations on the actual voyage. In addition, many facts and stories about her life are taken from the non-fiction work of biographers and other writers.

While most of the details of Montessori's life in the book are from history, I added the circumstances around the birth of her child, the struggle she has with this part of her life, and the closing letters written by her mother. I also changed the chronology of some events to suit the narrative (such as the earthquake in Messina). Finally, my interpretations of Montessori's observations, thoughts, and feelings throughout the story are purely fiction.

My intention in writing this book is to honor the brilliance and courage of an independent woman and to acknowledge the complex and deeply personal decisions she made at the time. We all face choices in our lives that cannot be undone, but rather shape us into who we will become. This tale is an invitation to live into those rather than to shy away from them, to honor them rather than to cast them as mistakes, for to change one thing is to change everything.

Prologue • 1913

Ribbons upon ribbons of water woven into a fine brocade; the view from the deck is so captivating that I have half forgotten where I am going. With so many fluffy clouds hanging above, I am transported back to stuffing pillows on the side porch, pulling the wool into long furls and pushing it into the casing.

The ship has only just left the home shores yesterday, yet somehow it feels as though we have been many days at sea. With little land in sight, there is only the terrain of the sea and sky to amuse me, and so I watch it all pass—the billowing interweave of sea swells and clouds—and think of you, my dear child. I think of you, even at fifteen, getting up on your tiptoes to see over the crowd, your hand in the air waving from the quay as the ship pulled away from the dock, with your changing face perched between joy and sorrow. I expect that is where my face is now as well, to have been so long without you and then to be parted again while still in this first year together.

America is ahead of me out there as Italy falls behind. Perhaps this un-interrupted time will be spent writing something. I have been changed through the having and losing of you, and I want to be worthy of your return, to spend the next years differently than the last.

I picture you now with your *nonno*, gnawing on a strip of meat, and I wonder what you make of all this. Relocated from your life in the country to live in the heart of Rome with so much bustle all around, and then within months, I am sailing off to America without you.

These past months, you have adjusted to life in the city rather well, with no noticeable sign of overwhelm except in the night. Still, the night terrors (which you continue to claim as leg cramps and nothing more) have you calling out, sometimes names I do not recognize, and this prompts me to lie awake in the night, turning over the events that led to our parting.

Today I discovered the typewriter in my ship's cabin that I am writing this on, and as I am tapping along on the keys writing this letter, it occurs to me to continue. Perhaps instead of a letter, I shall use this machine to unwind the past for you, Mario, the story of a time and place, for we are all of a particular time and place. Moving and acting from our point of origin, taking part in what will grow into the next time, and perhaps if we are determined, creating something lasting that will spread from place to place, just as right now I am headed across this wide ocean to bring my ideas to a new place. Perhaps by knowing your story, you too will bring thoughts and ideas forward in your own time long after I am tucked into the soil of Italy beside my own mother.

Chapter One • 1873

In absolute defiance, I am sitting on the kitchen counter with my arms crossed in a simple message of refusal. My red face is closed up like a shuttered house, the sound of my father's laughter raining down around me, and my mother's steady expression keeping me from erupting. My earliest memory; when I close my eyes now, I can see the scene as clearly as the brocade on the bedspread in this ship's cabin. Though I do not recall the details of my objection or how I came to be perched upon the counter, I remember that my papa's amusement caused a fury in me that only my mother could allay, coming quickly to me. Instead of lifting me off the counter, where I had somehow gotten myself, she pushed a chair close by and, in a comforting but serious voice, told me she understood my plight and believed I could solve it using the chair.

Though I was after something on the counter, this acknowledgment had a great effect. I took it as a challenge to traverse a dangerous passage and so set about adjusting my position in order to dangle myself down onto the waiting chair. I did this to pronounced satisfaction, beaming at my mother, angry tears on my cheeks now forgotten. She did nothing in response but offered a nod of recognition and used her eyes to indicate the next task—to move from the chair to the floor. I traveled with confidence and ease, having bested the more difficult maneuver from high counter to chair.

I share my earliest memory from childhood with you as a place for the story to begin. Here on a ship with a limited amount of paper, I shall need to stay with this opening for now and continue in faith that the tale I am to share will reveal itself regardless of point of origin. For, the story I am set to tell you was borne of that defiance and a direct result of the care and guidance offered to me by my parents throughout their lives. They parented me in a way I have not yet parented you: daily and with little interruption.

At that point in time, 1873 in Chiaravalle, when I was but three years of age, living a peaceful life in the country with my parents, I knew nothing of the recent unification of Italy nor the status of women. My life revolved around my mother and the daily cadence of our home, and I see from this distance the large impact that had upon the work I am now doing—how my trajectory, though not direct, was directed by those earliest years.

I am uncertain whether I was yet knitting as I was quite small at the time of this first recollection, but many memories of my mother involve knitting for the poor. This she did each and every day except Sunday, all the years of her life, and I joined her at some point, knitting with thick wooden needles, beginning with simple scarves.

The creation of my first scarf took my small hands the better part of a year, adding and then taking out rows as I learned. It was quite a wide contraption—the rows unnaturally long—so that one row was all I could manage in the time it took my mother's fast needles to produce much more. So swift were her fingers that, at times, I would sit, captivated by the clicking of her needles as they met and parted rhythmically, playing a song. This, too, may have contributed to my slow pace, and once or twice I even drifted off to sleep on my stool from the soothing sound of her needles, only to be woken as I pitched off onto the burgundy carpet. My landing would cause my father to laugh, startled by the thump of me from behind his newspaper.

My mother never laughed. She looked at me where I fell and noted whether the yarn had come loose from my needles in the fall, and if so, she would reach her hand out wordlessly and I would gather the knitting and bring it to her to rectify. While she was getting the loops properly back onto the needles, I would retrieve the yarn from wherever it had rolled and wind it carefully back into a proper ball.

I believe my father in no way meant to mock me on these occasions, and though it was a sting to my pride, each time I readily forgave him, crawling up into his lap and being held there while my mother repaired the situation. He would often read me snippets of the paper, amusing bits about people's ideas, and I would beseech him to keep reading even when my mother's hand appeared with my knitting righted.

He would gently put me back on my stool, and sometimes, if it was a particularly good bit, he would read the section through to the end while I was expected to resume my task. I remember the one about the telephone quite clearly and how I laughed then to think of people talking to someone who was not right there. The picture in my mind was of a helmet that went over my head attached to a long string that unwound like my yarn into another room in the house, where my father was also wearing a helmet attached to the cord. I had such a laugh at this that it caused him to stop reading, and I had to set my knitting down carefully and climb back up into his arms to see the picture in the newspaper.

Great was my disappointment when I saw what it really looked like, and I hung my head in shame that I had imagined something so different from what it truly was, sliding back down off my papa's lap and returning to my knitting with renewed seriousness and no more requests to hear his reading.

My mother noted this interaction yet said nothing, keeping her needles moving steadily. Later that night, as she was tucking me into bed with the lamp flame turned low so I could barely make out her face, she asked, "Tell me about your telephone." I described what I imagined adding more and more details until I was sitting up in bed, showing her over my head how the device would work. I must have gotten quite stirred up because my mother's hands landed on each of my shoulders in her find-your-feet gesture, gently but firmly pressing, so I returned to my body. She guided me back down under the covers, nestling me in just as I was explaining the way the sound would move through the cord.

Her hand across my forehead then made the ideas come slower until the words ebbed and ran out of me. I lay there in the lamplight waiting for her to say something, staring as always at the curtains my own *nonna* had sewn for me before she died. I remember little of her, but each night in Chiaravalle, I fell asleep by falling into those curtains, which to me resembled the entire universe of stars.

I recall we talked then about my embarrassment, how I had not quite gotten the same idea as what Mr. Meucci or Mr. Bell had made, even though theirs had cords too. My mother's hand kept soothing my forehead, getting lighter and lighter as we talked.

"Friendliness with error, Mimi, friendliness with error," she told me that night, a phrase I never forgot.

Chapter Two • 1874

Waves are lapping as I punch the keys to this obdurate typewriter. I have rolled a fresh sheet into its jaws because I can see a plate of sky through the porthole, bringing me back to a particular day. That particular day with you in the country continues to vibrate in my mind, and I recognize now that I hold it responsible for all that has happened since—a turning point—an occasion that prompted the seismic shift.

That day we were brought back together after such a long spell apart, the sun jagged across the field and clouds there to catch the colors of its departure, boasting peach, salmon, and a delicate lavender. How a sky can hold more than a canvas is proof enough of a God, though you have already made your beliefs known to your *nonno* and me, and I will be aware not to fill these pages with that which might underscore a lack of coordination, particularly since the purpose of this collection is to close the fault line, to bring us closer into alignment.

I have decided in the night: I will tell you the complete story. As I have already begun as far back in my life as I can remember, I will now continue and bring you to this moment, or really by the time I have written it all, it will be a future moment. I will bring you inside the unfolding of the person I am becoming, lay it bare for you to see. To judge if you must, but at least to know. One should know their origin story, and yours is deeply tucked inside of mine.

And so, I shall save the tale of shifting light in late afternoon, colors blooming skyward, your family assembled, tall trees as witness. I shall save it to come in its proper chronology here in this newly determined recital.

As I have mentioned, there is little paper in this ship cabin drawer, and so I shall not waste even a single sheet to start the next section. Instead, I shall draw my attention away from the porthole, which is a charming personal viewfinder for me, creating a circular frame around the scenery, which will soon be mostly sea and sky. I asked the captain earlier why windows on a ship are always round, and once he recovered from the question (it seems women passengers are not commonly curious about the ship's construction), he went into a long soliloquy about structural integrity that I enjoyed immensely. I only wish my notebook had been in my pocket to have captured more of the unique language he brought to the subject. Apparently, the ocean puts a great deal of pressure on the body of boats, and parallelograms tend to be weaker. Is that not a fascinating corroboration of the rules of geometry? Though it is true that the triangle gets the award for most stable there, with the circle trailing because of its exclusion from the world of polygons.

Interesting to note that I began that long section determined to take the attention off of the porthole, and instead, I focused on it entirely. I suspect the very construction of this missive will tell you more about me than perhaps I at first set out to reveal.

Yet in the revealing shall be the finding, and so we go to Chiaravalle and the small child I was then.

I spent my early years there until, at five, we moved from Chiaravalle to Rome. That seems a lifetime ago now, though it is clear in my mind that what I missed about home in that change was the routines so well established by place, routines such as my floor scrubbing.

I do not remember the day of starting with the tiles; my mother reports she set me to it when I was just three years old as a way to expend some of my energy. She had many tales to share about the antics of my early years, and I imagine this daily project may have begun as a redirection from other less productive ventures.

Yet to me, it was a privilege. Each day in Chiaravalle, I relished the morning ritual of scrubbing one tile on the kitchen floor. To my small hands, the large ceramic tiles were a sizable area to conquer, and the satisfaction of completing that task regularly was a staple, much like the daily egg pulled slowly from beneath the hen to become my breakfast. Yet, even more so was the routine of setting up to scrub the tile and cleaning up my tools afterward.

Perhaps it was my mother who shaped the exercise, but I recall it as fully my own—every step carried out without aid from another, my arms growing stronger through doing it. The cycle never varied, with each day finding the same series of events.

While I ate the hen's egg, I would study the floor beneath me. I always ate my first breakfast in the kitchen before Papa rose, so my "announcing voice," as he called it, might be contained by the thickness of the swinging door there. My father often remarked on the power of my voice and his idea that I should become a pastor, a vocation I considered several times throughout my life, though women have not yet done such a thing.

The kitchen floor held a design of tiles, each one full-sized enough for me to sit in it without spilling into the adjacent ones. My eyes would roam across them until they lit upon one in particular, often out of an interest in its individual color or design. Although once, when my mother asked how I chose, and I pointed out the unique characteristics of each one, she asserted that there was no pattern in the tiles at all and that they were solid in color. Rather than argue with something so obviously incorrect, I shook my head in sorrow that she was not able to see something of wonder in our very own kitchen. How, then, must she see the rest of the world? How, then, was she to enjoy the path to the grassy knoll or the view once we reached the hillside or when we lay down so that our heads were touching and we looked into the vast sky? My mother's eyes were broken, and the sadness of it made me cry.

"There, there, *mia cara*," she said, putting her morning teacup down onto the delicate saucer and patting me on the hand. The look on her face was so familiar to me that the tears stopped. It always felt as though everything was right in the world when I was in the presence of my mother. Writing this has tears appearing again, as though remembering it has dislodged a scab from a wound just beginning to cover over, the new layer of flesh barely attached, and the healing thus easily hampered. You were very kind to acknowledge her passing when you arrived; it saddens me that you never knew each other. Yet writing about her for you loosens that a bit. Had I known then what I know now, I would have surely stowed my stubbornness and yielded to her wishes to meet you.

The day after my mother asked that question, I began to scrub my tiles in sequence. I commenced in the corner by the pantry and went along the row of tiles to the right. When I first started the pattern, I began by the stove and was working to the left towards the pantry. It was only the second day of deciding this, but already my mother had noticed.

"Are you following a pattern now?" she asked in her quiet voice when I had stepped up on the stool she fixed for me to reach the sink. I had taken my little white pitcher from the low shelf in the pantry and was filling it to place it beside my white porcelain washing bowl and my tray with the scrub brush, soap, and cloth. I nodded seriously, perhaps a bit proud that I had thought of it and happy that she had noticed so quickly.

"Then, I would like to suggest that you begin with this one," she said, walking to the large, beautiful tile on the other side of the kitchen by the pantry door. I stepped carefully down from the stool, holding my pitcher with two hands as she had shown me—one on the smooth handle and the other cupped under the bottom—and walked to where she stood.

Excited by her attention to my project, I moved more quickly and little splashes of water pushed up over the edge of the pitcher, dripping down the sides to my hands. When I felt this, I slowed my feet immediately, hoping my mother would not notice the results of my haste.

We stood looking at the tile. The sparkles embedded in it glittered in the morning light. I wondered for a long while whether I had ever scrubbed this one. It did not seem familiar to me, and it was so far in the corner that I questioned then if I had ever even noticed it before. Such a shame to have neglected it!

I set the pitcher down carefully on the tile next to it, being sure to do it just as my mother had the first time—so slowly that there was no sound when it touched the floor. Then, without another word, I fetched my other supplies, laid them all out, and began to clean the beautiful glittering tile.

This daily ritual, moving along from left to right across the rows of tiles on the kitchen floor, filled my days in Chiaravalle, and I only wish I had asked my mother if she had intentionally set me to scrub as I would come to read. I have since included this wisdom in table washing and other exercises, and until remembering and transcribing the tale of the tiles here, I had entirely lost that origin, thinking I had come up with the idea on my own!

What I never lost, however, was the feeling of satisfaction gained from doing it. Gradual competence grew out of repetition until I felt an awareness of expertise in the work, one that occupied me with such pleasure that later, when we moved to Rome, with its brick-floored kitchen, I was temporarily lost without this activity.

This was also the case with my father's workshop.

My papa had a falling-down workshop on the far side of the chicken coop, and one day, when collecting the eggs, I watched him disappear inside of it, and I grew curious. Waiting patiently, as I had learned to do, I stood watching for him to emerge. When he failed to, I contrived to discover his purpose in there, pulling a dented bucket over under the window to stand upon. Laying my eggs carefully on the grass, I then balanced upon the pail and peered in through the dirty panes.

What I saw in there grew my eyes wide: there were carefully organized tools all along the wall, each with its own nail or hook and all dangling to create an appealing design. My father appeared deep in thought as he dismantled what appeared to be an old clock, turning pieces over in his hand as he removed them. Fascinated, I leaned in closer, and with that, the metal pail tipped. As I fell, I understood that I was headed for the eggs, and a small cry escaped my lips, followed by the crunch and squish of my landing on the near dozen.

Naturally, that brought my father from his shop, and he peered down upon me with anger rising in his eyes. Remaining entirely still, not even adjusting my side that lay directly across the broken eggs, I waited as though perhaps I could hide the calamity. I could feel the slippery innards moving beneath me while my father's face grew sunburnt. I shifted then to make my case, but as I spoke, it unleashed my father's fury in a long bellow that pulled my mother from the kitchen. "MARIA!" My name unfurled from his lips the way a heavy indigo cloud stretches across the field on a foul weather day.

Where this should have scared me, it instead enraged me, and I felt my hands clench around the innocent grass. "PAPA!" I shouted back at him with decades less force, but with great sincerity.

"WHAT WERE YOU DOING?" his voice dropped very little between shouting my name and this question.

"WHAT WERE **YOU** DOING?" I shouted back, sitting up without thinking about it.

At this point, my mother was on the scene, and our awareness of her dropped the volume of the conversation by decibels.

"Maria Tecla Artemisia Montessori, what is the meaning of this?" he demanded.

Somehow his use of my full name snapped me back into my frame, and I was aware of the eggs moving viscously down my back. "I wanted to see what you were doing." And with that, my voice weakened, and I thought I might cry.

"No" was all my mother said; but in that one small word, which my father took as agreement that I should not have been looking in the workshop window, I regained myself and looked directly at my father.

"Why on earth would you want to see what I am doing?" he asked.

"Because I would like to know how to fix things," I replied impulsively. Then, to my great surprise, a gust of wind came from inside him, and he burst out in a laugh. My relief was so great that instead of feeling the usual diminishment, I sprung to my feet and hugged him, leaving a trail of egg yolk behind.

That was my entrance into my father's private world of the workshop. From then on, he allowed me access, and over time he built me a series of steps to climb up to sit on the bench and watch his tinkering, for that is what he called it. I would not be surprised if you had a knack for fixing things, *mio caro*, for though your *nonno* was modest, he had a skill for taking something apart, understanding the flaw, and reassembling it so that it worked properly once again. Though I do not have this gift, I much enjoyed participating and became quite adept with tools.

The Chiaravalle library had precious few books in the children's section on tools, but the two they did have, I studied until I memorized them. For though the days were filled with activity, never did one go by that did not find me resting with my mother listening to her read. I knew it was time for this when she sat in the red chair in the parlor. This is the very same luscious stuffed chair with a sagging back cushion (made more so by my habit of sitting up there when no one else was in the room) that remains in our sitting room today. It has that wide bottom cushion so that I could easily nestle beside my mother without being on her lap—a position she felt was undignified.

Following our afternoon tea, she would move to the red chair and I to the bookshelf to select the day's adventure. There were those I loved to hear over and over, though this was tempered by the ones my mother favored. When I would bring her one to hear again and again that she did not prefer, she would say, "Let us savor that one for you to read to yourself," and I would put it in the special place on the shelf she had cleared for this purpose. I wonder now if, in fact, she was identifying those that would be easiest for me to read first on my own or keeping my interest for them ripe so I might seize them hungrily when the occasion came that I might be ready.

For there were days when the reading time ended, and I would finger the books in that collection, looking at the illustrations and trying to remember the story that went along through the pages. This created an eagerness in me to figure out how my mother was getting the story out of the letters, and with that, I believe my education began.

At that time, there was not a priority placed on the education of young girls, though, in my life in the country, this was not something I was aware of—my world revolving almost entirely around my mother, who had her own ideas and opinions on this topic.

These did not surface for me until I began to read on my own, and some weeks into it, my father took notice.

"Is she actually reading that book?" he asked my mother in a low voice.

We were in the after-dinner hour reserved for reading. My father, having read the newspaper during the afternoon's hand work time, would often read a large volume. As a young child, I would clamber up to see more closely the type bold and deep on the page that appeared to me then as small as ants in early spring traveling across the pantry floor.

That day I was on my knitting stool with a delicious volume of my own involving a naughty cat, and I heard him ask the question, though I did not take my eyes from the page.

"Yes," my mother replied simply.

There followed a silence filled with what I imagine was my father looking dumbfounded—though again, my eyes were trained to my page, and it is only through loving my father so well that I could picture this without seeing it. He was often as amazed by my mother as I was, and his expressive face broadcast that feeling.

"Maria," he said in a regular tone.

"You are interrupting her." This was a statement from my mother and also a direction. My mother was clever in her way of saying things so that you knew the right thing to do next.

"I believe she is simply looking, making no meaning of what she sees," my father said to her in reply.

"Mmmm" was my mother's response. This was another form of communication that allowed the other person to reflect on what they had said without either raising it up or taking it down. The person could do that for their own self, and my father must have been doing it during the silence that followed.

"Maria," he said again, but this time with a commanding tone that made my head lift. "Come here."

My mother did not raise her eyes from her own book through all of what followed.

First, he had me read out loud to him the words on the page I held open. Then, rubbing his chin, he was silent for just a moment, and though I very much wanted to continue the story on the next page, I waited for him to comfort his chin. Then he held forth his own book, which had been lying open on his lap, and pointed to the top of the page, indicating that I should take a go at reading his book. With the exception of a few very long words I stumbled over and could not make out, my father's book turned out to be not as difficult as I had imagined seeing its size and heft.

This prompted several things: a wind traveling from my father that was strong enough to ruffle my hair, a very small change in my mother's lips as they turned slightly up at the corners, her eyes still on her own story, and an untamed desire in me to read every volume in our house.

That night I began my quest and had a book from my parents' shelf held close to the lantern as stormy voices between them grew behind the wall of my bedroom. I could not make out the beginning of the conversation when their voices were customarily quiet so as not to wake me. However, as my father's voice grew in volume, I could hear his words clearly: "Why is it you must come up against me time and time again," offered more as a declarative statement than a question.

It is only in hindsight that their topic that night is clear to me. At the time, their argument fell into a category of disputes surrounding something vexing my father, and I wondered what had happened this time that so displeased him.

The next morning my parents announced our departure from Chiaravalle, and for a length of time, I associated their night quarrel with this decision. It was, in fact, related to my father's work, and our relocation to Rome was a result of his promotion to accountant first-class. For me, however, this was terrible news, and I was stricken to the point of running out of the house and hiding behind the rain barrel to cry.

I sat crouched there for some time until the tears had run out and my legs ached. I peered out from behind the barrel, thinking perhaps my mother would have come looking for me. Instead, I saw a lovely summer day with the early sun lighting the gardens in a way that showed the insects circling and looping in the shafts of light.

Mesmerized, I emerged and stood watching them move in their most natural and beautiful choreography, never crashing into one another, never tiring. As I studied them, I saw their wings and antennae more clearly, their individual shapes and sizes, and I longed to know all of their names.

"*Mammina!*" I called, reentering the house through the kitchen, and she turned from her work to me, perhaps expecting objections to my father's announcement but getting a request for a volume on insects instead.

We spent hours outside that last summer, and I absorbed them into my skin, my mneme, extracting the essence of them to carry with me into the new city. We picked and canned every type of berry that grew within miles of our home, as well as cherries, figs, and peaches, leaving behind the apples, pears, and quinces when we left. I sat upon the valise carrying the jars of fruit as we pulled away from the land that had raised me, still watching the insects loop over the garden, this time naming them as we went.

Chapter Three • 1876

Mr. Sam McClure has created quite the stir on board the SS *Cincinnati* as though I were a celebrity, and now, I must tuck into the cabin regularly to avoid being constantly approached and spoken at in English. Mostly I nod my head and smile as I have seen older people do when they cease to hear efficiently, but I find it taxing all the same. There is an emerging assumption that everyone speaks English and will adjust to their dominant tongue. Whether or not this is accurate, I do feel the rise of the defiance described in the previous section, one which has so far prevented me from learning much of that language.

As I reread that paragraph, I sound ungracious; I am very grateful for all that Mr. McClure has done to bring my ideas to America. He, with the backing of the previously mentioned Mr. Bell himself! Astounding to think that I was a small child as he was launching his work into the world, and now, he turns to support me in launching mine.

Of course, I understand that people's enthusiasm is important if we are to reach American children with this method. Nonetheless, I find myself preferring the solitude of my cabin, where I can take off my hat and my outerwear and get comfortable until Mr. McClure sends a message urging me out. I am certain you can imagine this, *mio caro*, having met Mr. McClure not long ago and knowing personally of his persistent nature.

This morning I was up at five o'clock and went out on deck into the cold and windy air. I was all alone but for the last stars in the sky and the moon reflected in the waves. After sunrise, the coastlines of Africa and Spain were in sight, and by eight o'clock, we were so close to Gibraltar that we could see the homes of Gibraltar and Algeciras. Many ships passed through the Strait, and I could feel the transition as we sailed. It is very exciting to be entering the wide ocean, and I have been thinking intensely of you and how you have also made the passage from the calm beginnings in the country, enjoying a simple life, now into the open ocean of life with me.

In spite of my resistance, a word I learned at dinner last evening turns in my mind: *momentum*. There is an elegance to the simplicity and directness of this word that very much appeals. One word is so pleasing, when we must use "*quantità di moto*," which is instead a jumble of *ttttts*. The word *momentum* connects to its meaning—there was a catalyst that set something in motion that gains force as it proceeds. Its root is Latin, from *movere* or "to move," and this has made me aware that both the ship and I are gaining momentum, the ship in the journey to America and me in the telling of this story, which is yours.

And how lovely to have found momentum with my tale, as I am feeling such a connection to both your journey and the transition in this sea voyage. There is something about marking the change from protected waters into a vastness, an area so large that one might even feel lost for a bit at the start. We are but stardust. Specks on this speck of a planet.

For me, though the city differed from the countryside, I unexpectedly took to the expansion of my worldview, enjoying the companionship of the other children in the apartment building and the many unfamiliar sights and sounds both in my neighborhood and when we traveled about. I had spent the first five years largely with my mother, learning how to do things by watching her. Now I had many more people to watch and learn from.

In the new apartment, my room was no longer adjacent to my parents, and so perhaps there was a quarrel that I missed, but within the first week in Rome, my parents ceased to speak to one another, and I knew something was amiss.

"Maria, would you please pass the butter?" my father would say, though the butter was just beside my mother and much easier for her to reach. This, after my mother had set out only two place settings for the meal, requiring my father to go into the kitchen to retrieve his own plate and cutlery, storming about until we heard the clatter of silverware and the breaking of a dish.

"That is enough!" he shouted in his fierce voice, storming from the dining room, shaking his head furiously and nearly kicking the swinging door to the kitchen as he retreated with his supper.

Eventually, this evening theater routine came to an end when my mother and I returned from fitting me for a new outfit, and I walked proudly up to my father to show him how refined I looked. His eyes moved from me to my mother, who was taking off her coat and hanging it in the closet.

"So, you have enrolled her anyway?" he asked, his voice growing hot.

Just the slightest tilt of her head to answer him, and then she spoke to me, holding her hand out. "Come, *tesora*, let's take your uniform off so it will be ready for you tomorrow."

The next day I began primary school on Via di San Nicolo da Tolentino, and within a few days, my parents were speaking again as though nothing had happened.

Now, you might think that for one who so adores learning, I would see this opportunity to attend school with the other children from the apartment building as immensely rewarding. Quite to the contrary, following the initial excitement of wearing a uniform and walking to the school, I found it an intolerable cage.

The other children were not yet reading, so we spent all of our time learning letters. The teacher felt it was her duty to keep us all together, and so she had us repeat and copy letters for months all the way through the fall and into the heart of winter.

Those early days I sat at my small desk watching the sky outside the window, missing my grassy knoll and regretting the move to Rome. That was until part way into the year when I learned to bring a small book that fit on my lap as *Sig*. Rapport, the librarian, had suggested. From there forward, I was much more content to wait for the others to put their letters together into words and their words together into sentences.

This was true in *donneschi* as well, where none of my classmates had yet held knitting needles. I taught them casting-off after school on the apartment stoop, though what I wished to be doing was playing stickball with the boys. That was something I had never seen before, and I very much wanted to try, but when I talked them into letting me join, I was so unskilled that they would not pick me to be on their team any longer. There was one boy taller than the rest, Rollo, who made decisions for the group, and if anyone even looked at me standing there waiting for sides to be picked, he would bellow, "She is too bad to play," at which point they would choose someone else.

In the early days of school, I sought out the thoughts and ideas of my teacher, watching her face closely as I had my mother's, but when I found no response there, I soon ceased. The teacher, who seemed over-worked and harried, paid me no mind. I went on to complete the first grade without incident.

The major influence of that first year in Rome was finding the library and meeting *Sig.* Rapport.

My mother found this building like the birds of prey would find the voles in the garden, drawn to it and swooping on it with ferocious hunger. The day we walked in for the first time stands out as it was among the best presents I have ever received, and I believe my mother constructed this outing on the day of my sixth birthday for just that reason.

"Where are we going?" I asked my mother as she set her hat on her head and gathered her bag.

Her face betrayed nothing, and we were out the door, my hand in hers with the smells of Rome greeting us as we descended to the sidewalk. We traveled at my mother's customary no-nonsense pace, with my five steps to her one, making our way through the streets as though we had lived there a long while. At the time, I did not question this as, in my mind, my mother knew everything and there was nothing beyond her. However, as I write it to you now, I am taken by her strong sense of direction, always guiding us, and by her quest for us to be in the world without flinching.

When we arrived at an impressive building, my mother announced it was the library. We stood staring at its size—in awe that it was entirely filled with books. I followed my mother's gaze to the foundation, where she seemed to inspect its position on the ground.

We stood looking for a bit, with my thoughts traveling in an effort to understand why we were looking there and what we might be looking for. Finally, my curiosity got the better of me, and I asked quietly, "What are we looking for?"

"Signs of sinking," she replied. "I read of a library constructed for a large number of volumes. When the building was complete, there was a celebration planned for the conclusion of the book installment. On that day, as the town assembled inside, the unexpected extra weight of all the books and the people was so great that the building sank into the ground."

The Biblioteca Nazionale Centrale di Roma had been inaugurated in March, just prior to our arrival, and so, though I did not know it, the library was new for everyone, not just for me. It was our good fortune that the architects had thought to fortify it for the weight it would bear when it held the heavy books and reference material as well as the visiting public.

There in the entryway, our hands locked together, we took in the vastness, the grand difference from the Chiaravalle library. When my mother sniffed, I did as well, practically tasting the old volumes housed there, the lovely dry bark and musty smell that can take you places you didn't know you wanted to go.

It was there in that very building on my sixth birthday that I found the book that changed my life, and it was quite by accident.

Once we crossed the threshold to greet the librarian, we had an orientation to the design and organization of the structure. This was my first meeting of *Sig*. Rapport. He led us around on the first day and, over the following years, was the one who seamlessly guided me through the changes in my literary appetite. On that day, he did something no one else in Rome had done. He came around from behind his desk to greet my mother, and then he squatted down so that his face was at the same level as my face and greeted me just as properly.

The feeling was quite inexplicable at the time; all I knew was that I felt he saw my correct size when he looked into my eyes, and I knew his size as well.

Then he stood up to begin the tour, and the three of us walked through the immense building together. Despite its grandness and the fact that it was the largest structure I had ever been in, I felt very safe there—on that day and all the days that would follow.

We went about from floor to floor with *Sig*. Rapport telling us what each area was designed for and how it was organized. He asked both my mother and me many questions as we went along, and I was aware of how unusually open and responsive my mother was, as though he were a relative instead of a stranger. Usually, she held back. She said less than those she spoke with, and she seemed to only say words that would matter, not simply ones to fill the spaces in the conversation. If a social conversation flagged, my mother would instead lead it to something far more interesting. She had a way of doing that. And yet I had not seen her in this type of reciprocal conversation before with anyone but me.

Well into the visit, we arrived at a room that had another room inside of it made of all glass and lined with large books. *Sig*. Rapport must have noticed how overcome I was by the sight of this and how much I instantly longed to be inside that glass room. Yet he was patient. He was patient and allowed time for us to fully appreciate the room, to build up the wanting until the wish made its way to my lips.

"May we enter?"

"This is the Research Room. It holds all the most precious volumes in the library that are never to be loaned, only to be enjoyed in this room." He paused as I absorbed this information.

My mother, who had been nodding as though she knew of such a room before, waited also and then asked, "Is special permission required?"

"It is," he replied, and I felt my heart sink. It had only been a week in school, but already I realized special permission was as rare as a sighting of the blue morpho butterfly.

"And I imagine then there is a key?" my mother went on.

"There is," *Sig*. Rapport answered.

And there we stood on the outside of the glass room of special books that only those with special permission and a key could ever read.

Just as I was feeling tears forming, *Sig*. Rapport squatted down again to address me directly. "We give permission to those who are responsible."

I nodded without answering as a way to keep the tears to the corners of my eyes and no further.

"If a person is known to be very responsible, then they are free to visit the Research Room," he said, reaching inside his suit jacket, feeling along the collar of his crisp shirt, and drawing out a skeleton key strung along a chain around his neck.

The key was long and intricate. My hands began to tingle, a sign I came to know as being present during important moments, though this was the first time I noticed and remembered it. The sensation created a desire for my hands to reach for the key. He stood then to ask my mother if I was in school, taking the key with him as he rose.

They talked at length about education, a topic that had become familiar to me from the many conversations between adults in neighborhood, as it was as much a subject of dispute then as it is now.

As much as I tried to be patient, the temptation of the glass room, the books, and the key was all too much for me, and I began squeezing both of their hands with increasing urgency until I clutched them both with all the strength in me uttering the word *please*.

This brought both of them to their senses, and the return seemed to be funny to them, for they both laughed, and then it was my birthday again with the feeling that I was about to get a huge present.

Sig. Rapport let go of my hand and, approaching *Sig*. door, leaned down and fit the key into the keyhole, turned the glass knob, and opened the door. When he turned back to us, his face was alive—eyes lit, lips wiggling about. I walked to the open room like a magnet, towing my mother behind me.

Inside, standing close to all the books I could see but never take home, my tingling hands reached for the large volume open on a book stand above me. I used the tips of my toes to allow me a peek at the displayed book. *Sig*. Rapport, seeing the height differential, cleared his throat and pointed to a stool set by the tall shelf at the back. I dutifully walked to the stool and carried it as my mother had taught me, bringing it to rest in front of the stand that held the book. When I climbed up, I could see pages holding illustrations of stars and, as I learned in the coming weeks, planets, constellations, and galaxies.

I visited this book on every trip to the library for the first years we lived in Rome. There came a time when *Sig*. Rapport was busy, and he would silently hand me the key to the Research Room and return to his work. This left me free to study every part of this volume of secrets, for by then, I had memorized all the illustration pages and had set out to read about our world, how it began and what followed, leading to the beginning of life on our planet.

Naturally, this shaped my perspective on the small life I was living with my parents. I was no longer inside just my own life, but living inside the history of the universe. I was an active part of the story, and it was clear to me then that if each living thing had a contribution to make, then I myself had one as well.

The other children in the apartment building did not yet know about the library and had not visited the room of extraordinary books and so would plead with me to tell them another true story of the stars, the grand explosion, the way matter instinctively pulls together. There was one doubter, Rollo, the stickball boy, who would challenge me, saying, "That is not true—you are making that up." As a result, I began to create experiments to show them all that it was real.

The first one I came up with was after Rollo declared that particles did not attract. Right at that moment, I began tearing bits of paper and dropping them across the top of a puddle in the street. All the children crowded around as I did this, and at first, the paper bits just floated there. "See–you are wrong!" Rollo called, standing up from the puddle like the experiment was over and had failed. The other children followed him, stepping back as well, except for one, Simon, a smaller boy who, until now, had been at the edge of the play and not part of it.

What I think of now is how unfazed I was by this, how entirely certain I was that the book was true and right. Bent over that puddle I did not move a muscle. The other children, curious now to see what Simon and I were watching, moved back in around the puddle. Slowly but slowly, the paper bits moved toward each other until, ever so gradually, they came together in one clump. "Particles attract," I announced quietly, and from that day forward, if there was a dispute, the little group of children no longer looked at Rollo. They looked at me.

Simon, who had been regularly diminished by Rollo and thus taken much teasing to the point of being an outcast, on that day came to be a bit of a research assistant. He had a limp from some condition I now wish I knew the name of, but at the time, I only knew that though his body seemed weak, his mind was strong. He could not play stickball and join the games in the street, but rather hung at the sides and watched. I noticed this at the outset of my arrival in Rome, but it was not until the day of paper in the puddle that he came into view as both an ally and a collaborator.

Simon did not go to school with the rest of us and, as a result, did not yet know how to read. "He is an idiot," Rollo would say when Simon's words would get stuck on the way out. I grew more and more aware of Rollo's merciless attacks on someone of unequal size and girth, watching as Simon absorbed these insults, seemingly unaffected. Eventually, I went to talk to my mother about it.

"What is wrong with Simon?" I asked her one evening as we were doing the dishes.

"Why do you think something is wrong?" she asked without turning around.

I began to explain to my mother who Simon was when she broke in. "Yes, I know who Simon is, and I am wondering why you think there is something wrong."

Her uncharacteristic interruption surprised me. I thought about her question through the end of my drying duties and finally came up with, "He is different."

"Yes, he is, *mia cara*, and difference is necessary for beauty." She turned and dried her hands on my dish towel, shifting to look right into my eyes. "Think of your tiles. Would you have liked them as well if they were all exactly the same?"

Thus began my new mission to find where difference created beauty. There was evidence everywhere. My favorite chicken, *Crema*, had looked entirely different from the other hens; my favorite marble was not one color but a swirl resembling Mars; and my favorite book in the library was the largest volume that was one of few that could not be checked out. All different. All beautiful to me. As I write this, I wonder now if this idea unconsciously fueled my veracity to be a girl where there were only boys.

The beginning years of school were meant to be my only years, as girls completed their education at eight years old. At the time, people believed girls needed to be home learning daily how to run a household so they would be fit to do so in their own marriages.

My mother had other ideas. She was not hesitant to be direct with me in these matters, as she had been in other matters when I was small. Over those three years, she made a particular point of placing volumes in my hands that held stories of women who made appreciable changes, brave and determined women who did what they needed to do to use the gifts they had been born with. From Joan of Arc to Elizabeth Blackwell, I read about people who became my heroes. I have continued to revere the bold as I have aged, including Helen Keller, whom I have included at the start of my book on this method of education I am traveling to America to discuss.

This reading about the universe and the clever women inhabiting it went on until the time of the completion of my elementary program. Then came the time for me to enroll in another school that went into the higher grades, a school that ceased to prepare me to run a house-hold because the students there were only boys. Boys did not need to learn how to run a household because they merely lived there. Everyone knew boys did not run things.

What boys did was learn about states of matter, trebuchets, and land and water forms, and so it interested me greatly to continue my education.

I do regret how much my desires caused strife within my household from my early memories through the course of my parents' lives, with my mother, in her quiet determination, pushing past my father's wish-es, followed by his outrage and resentment. In those days, with the role clarity of running the household, my father's injured pride confused me, and I wondered if he did not know or understand that it was my mother's job. He went off to his work, and my mother never attempted to dictate what should happen there. Why, then, was my father's pride injured when my mother made her decisions at home?

As for me, I was not interested in running a household, and my mother's observation of this meant that enrolling me in a "boys' school" was the right and natural next step. It confounded me that my father, who spoke intelligently on so many topics, read such large and interesting books, and worked as a respected civil servant, could not see this point as clearly.

Your *nonno*, though a kind man, was not the most forward-thinking one, and this you will come to know as you live with him longer. He can be conservative in his views, both politically and personally, though his sharp mind and generous heart continue to push him to accept and forgive those he loves. Whatever you choose and whoever you become, do not fear that your *nonno* will leave you, for despite his noisy claims, ultimately, he allows his heart to decide, and his heart will always choose you.

This type of objection happened when I completed school and sought to continue. My father staged a brief protest that lasted about as long as the disturbance when Ernestina Prola got her driver's license and all of Italy was in an uprising. Do you remember that? You were only nine at the time, but I am certain word got out to the country as it was such a scandal that an Italian woman should drive a motorcar!

My recollection of those next years was of my daily interface with new information without the distraction of the handwork, which, though I enjoyed, I did not miss. What I did miss was my time on the stoop with the other children, playing and talking, and my time with Simon. Shortly after the paper experiment, I spent time with him on how to read, and over the years, I grew to find him my greatest intellectual companion. He had a curiosity and thirst that I didn't find in other children from the neighborhood, and it aggrieved me that his family did not see this and did not enroll him in school, perhaps imagining him incapable. Thus, I went off to the boys' school of engineering with only Rollo, leaving Simon and the other children in the neighborhood.

Perhaps it results from the rising sea storm and the rocking of this ship as the waves grow larger that I am called out of the blue to remember with some clarity the illness that took me when I was ten. I wish *Mammina* was still alive so that I could turn to her now in this ship's cabin and ask her what ailed me then, and she could have filled in my hazy details of that episode. There have been many times these past weeks when I have had the idea to ask her something and felt renewed sorrow over the loss of her.

It is really through her tale of this time that I remember it, though the heat that gathered in my body without abating and the many times she needed to change the bedclothes comes back to me even as I write about it, for the fever lasted days and days. In my mother's telling, just at the height of the illness, when she worried I would not survive it, I opened my eyes and told her, "Do not worry, Mother, I cannot die; I have too much to do," though as I read that off the page now it seems fairly preposterous.

I include it here so that you will know that I have always been busy with much to accomplish. Before you came to Rome, it seemed that going to America would be an important step in moving the work forward. I am grateful to you for your encouragement while I confess to being still unsure whether the decision was the right one for us. Perhaps if there is another voyage there, you will accompany me? At fifteen, is travel something that intrigues you? You seemed interested when Mr. McClure spoke of his many voyages and the places he described. I watched your eyes light up as he drew the tale for you.

Did you know that Mr. McClure wrote to me extensively before he turned up on our doorstep the week after you yourself arrived? It was such an unusual series of events in a short period of time starting at my mother's death, moving into your arrival, and then the spontaneous visit of Mr. McClure. He had written a year earlier, and after quite a few exchanges, I had agreed to go to America. Then when I received your letter, I wrote to him and told him it was no longer possible. When I heard nothing in response, I imagined that his enthusiasm had been affected by time and distance and that he had also thought the better of bringing this Italian woman who speaks but a few words of English to his country.

The evening he knocked upon our door when we had just entered the sitting room for reading after dinner, the weather had turned. You carried the tea tray with a blend of herbs you had brought from the country that tied both of us to the farm in smell and taste and had just set it down when the door knocker sounded. We all stopped moving and looked at one another, wondering who that could be. Then your *nonno* shrugged and went to open the front door.

Mr. Sam McClure stood on the step in the dark of night wearing all black, with his hat pulled down over his ears as though he were cold. He stood with an older woman wearing no coat who introduced him. "This is Mr. Sam McClure. He has come from America to speak in person to Dr. Montessori and wishes for me to translate the conversation. May we come in?"

I think your *nonno* was so struck by the straightforward introduction that, without speaking, he opened the door and half bowed while sweeping his arm toward the inside of the house in an exaggerated gesture, as if he wanted to be sure Mr. McClure understood his response. This brought the visitors forward into the entryway, where Mr. McClure stomped his feet a few times as though he were knocking snow off of his shoes. You and I looked at each other briefly and then back to watch the arriving party as your *nonno* took Mr. McClure's coat and once again gestured grandly for them to enter the sitting room.

At that point, I stepped forward and introduced myself to the kind woman, asking her name and greeting her before receiving Mr. McClure, who regarded me all the while. "Welcome, Mr. McClure. Might I offer you some tea?" His translator repeated my salutation and inquiry in a quiet tone so that he might understand my words without her speaking for me.

"That would be wonderful, thank you," he replied. With that, I took the tea tray and returned to the kitchen to make a larger pot of something more expected for guests. While the kettle re-boiled, I put a few biscuits and dried apricots on a plate for good measure.

Relieved to have had reason to leave the room, I stood still for a moment and took a few deep breaths. Mr. McClure had come from America! As I said, he had written repeatedly, entreating me, and was quite articulate, his vision compelling about the need for a new form of education for the young children of America. While I was intrigued, your arrival in Rome had changed all that, and my desire to pursue such a journey had evaporated. So, this was his response to my letter!

As I rounded the corner to reenter the sitting room with the refreshed tea tray, I heard your *nonno*'s voice say, "He is the boy Montessori," and my mind ran around itself, imagining the question this was an answer to. All the while realizing that I had exited the room without introducing you, forgetting my manners entirely, and that I had left you to fend for yourself. I felt a burn on my face then that caused me to pause before reentering the room. In this momentary gap, your *nonno*'s words were translated, and, after a brief hesitation, Mr. McClure repeated, a bit too enthusiastically, "Of course! He is the boy Montessori!"

At that point, vowing never to leave you unintroduced again, I pushed myself back into the sitting room and fully interrupted the moment with the tea service, pouring and passing cups on saucers, followed by the sugar bowl and so on. This allowed everyone to focus on something warm, which had a palliative effect on the group.

"So, Dr. Montessori," Mr. McClure began once everyone had commented on the tea and biscuits and settled into their respective places around the room. Without knowing it, you had taken up your *nonna*'s chair beginning on the first night, and it did me good to see you there then, sitting tall with your back straight and your feet solidly on the ground. It caused me to notice that my own feet were tapping and shifting as though expecting to flee, and I quieted them as best I could.

"So, Mr. McClure," I replied with a smile that I hoped was warm.

He started in before I had the opportunity to complete my opening thought. "I received your communication about the trip to America, and I have made the voyage here to change your mind." As soon as the translator completed this sentence, your *nonno* coughed and then took a sip of tea as though a cookie crumb had traveled down the wrong track, though I knew he was responding to this ill-chosen opening by Mr. McClure. A trait that your *nonno* and I share is that we find it difficult to change our minds. Once we have determined to do, or in this case, to not do, something, we are more or less a train on a track or, as your *nonna* would say, a cannonball fired from a cannon. It is hard to get us to change course.

I smiled and nodded, sipping my tea and leaving him to say whatever he had come to say next. This he did for the next three hours, recounting the need for Montessori schools in America and the importance of a voyage to speak about the method. And again, the next day and the next, until we had all begun to find business far away from the front door so we would not be the one required to answer it. At each turn, I found my resolve in your face—one I cherish and found I could not look upon enough. Though his argument was compelling, Mr. McClure could not convince me to leave you for a journey in the fall when you had only just arrived in winter.

Then came the night after his third visit. As the door clicked behind them, *Nonno* waited there as though he were counting their steps down the front before hollering, "That is enough, Mimi!" This was the first time you heard him address me using this name and in this tone, and you moved as though to go upstairs. "Mario, stay," your *nonno* demanded, and you stopped in your tracks. "Mimi, Mario and I have determined that this foolishness must end, and we have booked your passage to America."

My face must have given away the rush of feelings that erupted in me then—my fury that he would decide for me, my anguish to imagine leaving you, and my longing to have the method reach more children—for he interjected as if to intercept my response. His voice began booming and then decreased in volume as he spoke, as though he were winding down or running out of petrol. "Yes, we had to put a stop to it.

Your mother is no longer here, and so we must sort this through together. You may say whatever you like as objections to both my declarations and to my right to make them, and I will listen. But before you do, listen to the boy."

He stepped aside then, and our eyes fell on you as you spoke plainly, in a few words. The ones that continue to go through my mind are the ones you ended with. "You do not have to worry about me."

In hindsight, I can see how very unfair this was to put you in that position, and I feel hot about the ears as I write this.

I just yielded to the increased sway of the ship for a few minutes so I could return to typing without causing so many errors from a disrupted state. At that time, too, I was in a disrupted state—you looking at me so earnestly, agreeing with your *nonno* that it was the best course of action. And what have I forgotten? Was there a catch in your voice as you said this? Was it your true estimation or one informed by your esteem of your *nonno*? Or the goodness instilled in you from the farm and the influence of the Accardi family's generosity? Was it my own buried eagerness to move the work across the sea that affected my judgment? These are the questions I turn over and over as the vessel moves further away from you.

Now the sea is pitching about, and the typewriter has begun to slide from one side of this small desk to the other, setting the bell to clang each time, though I have not completed a row. I wonder what is happening above, and though I hesitate to leave the story now, for fear I shall lose my nerve to write it, I feel I must understand the lurching of the vessel. When I return, I will share about the crossroads in my schooling that came when I was twelve and needed to choose between the classical route and the technical one. To my papa's exasperation, I selected the technical one as the work of numbers fascinated me, as well as understanding how all things operated. I thought at the time that he would understand and approve, given his world was entirely filled with numbers and we had spent many hours together taking things apart as we sought to discover what made them work. However, he managed to raise the roof with his usual objections that my mother eventually soothed into disappearance. Indeed, I do wish my mother's hand were here now as the ship's constant movement left me less able to sleep than I would like last night, though it has been good for these pages, which are stacking up on the desk beneath the paperweight in quite a satisfying manner.

Chapter Four • 1890

I lingered up on deck a good long while this morning, mostly in gratitude for the fine day and also as a way to clear myself of the hours in the night tilting, hearing the passengers below me in the more rudimentary conditions moaning from the ship's hull as though losing at arm wrestling. Perhaps when land mammals are taken so far from shore we have a primitive fear for our lives, believing there is an ever-decreasing possibility that we could return to dry land on our own steam. That, and the sight of sharks and other creatures that could quickly interrupt our journey home. Then, when you add mounting wind that buffets the vessel holding us safe, we are all surely moving from our most rudimentary thinking.

Yet up on the deck, breathing in the sweet salt air, it seems implausible that the night wind we felt could have moved such a solid vessel so rigorously. As much as I was glad you were safe at home this past rocky night, on this day, I would like you to be beside me, *mio caro,* to link my arm through yours and discuss the fine array of clouds that have collected as meringues along the horizon.

The very thought of this has me pulling a ginger candy out of my pocket, unwrapping it cautiously, putting it into my mouth, and putting the wrapping paper safely back into my pocket. Astonishing that I have had these in my pocket all along and only this morning thought to have one, as ginger is a helpful aid to the upset system.

The upset system is the right segue to take you to the next part of my life, and that would be the adventure of medical school. Though my last pages imply that I will embellish my time at the technical school, there is very little that I feel called to relay now that the sun is shining so brightly and with such promise. Instead, now, I will take you to a scene that occurred a bit later.

"Tell me what you know about dismemberment," the Dean stated. In it, there was a question so intriguing that I did not realize until much later, as I told my mother and watched her face, that he had meant to provoke me. In that moment of the interview, however, I was delighted that if accepted into the school, these would be the terms I was entering into. They had yet to offer a place to a woman, but that seemed no real reason not to go through the process. I had made it through the numerous examinations and spontaneous writings on various topics, and I found myself at the step which no woman had yet done—the personal interview.

I sat with my legs uncrossed beneath my dark dress, both of my feet on the ground, as I had been taught never to do. This, however, was how I naturally sat when there was not a person who insisted upon a proper position, and for me, it established a feeling of being quite prepared for anything, and with a large desk between us, it seemed unlikely to be noted. So, when the *Sig.* posed the question about dismemberment, I easily launched into discussions of previous dissection experience and my great interest in applying the same skills to a human cadaver.

What followed then was most surprising as he stood and invited me to observe just such an activity. Again, my mother's eyebrows raised as I told her this part, though, at the time, I was further enthralled by the opportunity and in no way perceived it as a test. We entered directly into a room where the other medical students stood around a body, draped with what looked to be a sail taken from an old ship. My hands began to tingle.

All heads turned when I entered and then froze, looking at me as if they had intended to glance but then became unable to return their eyes to the corpse. My host seemed pressed to explain our intrusion and so announced, "This is *Sig.ra* Montessori, who has applied to the medical school, wishing to enroll in the forthcoming term."

They made no movement whatsoever, as though they had achieved simpatico with the cadaver before them.

To help them back into motion, as I very much wanted to see the promised dismemberment, I reached out my hand to the nearest gentleman, who reflexively extended his in return, though I could see straight away that with his gloves on this was not the proper gesture within the Anatomy Laboratory. "*Buongiorno*," I greeted him, and his face remained quite blank as though I were the body reaching up in greeting. "What is your name?" I prompted.

This led to each one coming forward, bowing slightly to replace taking my hand in theirs, and reporting their name. The first to approach introduced himself as Giuseppe Montesano, and his gaze was the most direct and unwavering as he bowed, his clean-shaven face open unlike the rest, who looked elsewhere in a motion of non-greeting. The last man, perhaps because he was furthest away at the start of this, was Rollo, from the old neighborhood, and he looked over me rather than at me as he reintroduced himself. I would not have recognized him immediately as his black hair, though still thick and curly, was now tamed (no longer headed off in all directions), perched atop his man's body. It was his malevolent eyes and the roughness of his demeanor that led me back to the boy he had been.

All of this happened in the shortest time, and then, relieved, they returned to consider their work. When I did not immediately leave the room, they began shifting about until *Sig.* Montesano brought them back to where they had left off by asking about the exposed organ. Some glanced behind at me and then at the door, but in a short time, the procedure demanded their attention over me.

I will tell you now that it was utterly fascinating, and as the procedure (as inexpertly done as it was) progressed, I became so engrossed that at one point, I leaned in, earning a stern look from the man before me who had mumbled his name upon introduction to the point of being unrecognizable.

When I left the room, I knew much more about the human body

simply from observing. I remembered what my mother had coached me on before coming and bridled my enthusiasm in the ensuing discussion though it was a constant effort to keep my hands from moving, my voice from rising, and my body from lifting off the chair I was reseated in following the visit to the Anatomy Laboratory. Something was moving through me, drawing me like a hunger toward what I had seen, and it was only through great self-restraint that I could manage the rest of the interview without spilling over myself, a vessel filled to overflowing with the desire to know more.

In relaying the details to my mother, I allowed myself the full telling—hands flying as I paced and exclaimed. The concern in her eyes grew, prompting me to reassure her I had not responded in this manner to the gentleman offering the interview. Her eyebrows tilted in her skeptical-yet-willing-to-be-convinced look at this, and I went on with my telling, reveling in all that I had seen and heard in the Anatomy Lab until I had exhausted myself and plopped into my chair.

The day the rejection letter arrived, I was in a jovial mood, as we had just come in from the market with baskets piled up with delights, so I exercised no caution when tearing open the wax seal. The words "We regret to inform you" stung as entirely disingenuous. Defeat was something I did not take lightly, and when I crumpled into the kitchen chair, my mother ceased to unpack the hampers, laid the wheel of cheese down on the table, and placed her hands on each of my shoulders in her find-your-feet gesture. From there, she could see the heading, "University of Rome Medical School," and the opening words of the letter.

We remained in that position for some time, digesting the news, listening as the hall clock ticked and the minutes moved away from the moment of rejection. When I finally looked up at her, she asked, "Tea?"

I nodded.

My mother then heated the kettle and laid out the setup before us. "What would you like to do next?" she asked. This was her standard question whenever I reached an impasse.

I remember once in the fields of Chiaravalle when I had built a nest and then entered it from the hayfield side. I enjoyed my time in the nest. However, when I attempted to exit out the opposite side, it was thick with brambles. My mother came along to find me frozen, unwilling to move for the tearing that the thorns made on my bare arms and legs.

She knelt down, considering my position. "What would you like to do next?" she asked.

Or the time in Rome when I convinced all the children from the apartment to go up onto the roof to see the clouds, and Rollo didn't mind the door, so it closed behind us, locking us up there. This set the others into a panic, but fortunately, our flat was on the top floor and so a plan came easily to mind. I had the boys take off their belts, which we strung together and used as a safety line so that I might hang over to look in the window and wait for *Mammina* to appear.

Despite the years that have passed since then, the remembrance of her face as she saw me hanging there that day has me laughing as I write this to you. She quickly gained her composure, however, and without hesitation asked out the open window, "What would you like to do next?"

So, you see that the question was her way of honoring that though my reach may have exceeded my grasp, I was perfectly capable of figuring out a solution, nonetheless.

The ship seems to be listing to the side now, and the typewriter is refusing to stay in one spot on the desk. In addition, my stomach is not finding this part of the journey agreeable, and so I must hasten to complete this page.

What I set out to tell you was about your *nonno*, and so I will focus on that for now. I anticipated he would be relieved to discover I had not been admitted and that there would be an end to what he seemed to feel was my foolishness. Yet when I told him the news that evening, his eyes moved to a spot on the wall behind me and his shoulders stiffened. I had only seen my father behave in this way one other time in my memory then, and it was when we first moved to Rome. We were out on the street when a man he worked with stopped to speak with him without making eye contact with my mother. Given my short stature, I was not in the adult's sightline and so had no expectation that people would look at me, which gave me the opportunity to observe without being noticed. What I saw that day was my father's attempts to include my mother in the conversation and the man's silent refusal to do so by continuing to address only my father. It was at my father's third attempt, turning and gesturing to my mother, saying, "My wife knows much more on this topic," that it occurred. The man continued to regard my father rather than following his gesture to my mother. My father's shoulders stiffened, and his gaze shifted over the man's ear.

Two weeks following my receipt of the rejection letter, as I was still working out my next plan of action, another letter arrived—this time, a letter of acceptance. It was written as though the first never existed, and I stood staring at it, rereading the words: "It is with profound pleasure that we welcome you as a member of the class of 1894 to the University of Rome Medical School."

My mother entered the parlor to find me there with the paper in my hand. "What is it, Mimi?" she asked with concern in her voice, running her hand up my arm. I realize now that, because of the shock, I must have looked as though it were bad news. I handed the letter to her to read, which she did quickly as though gulping it.

Her eyes rose to meet mine, and smiles instantly broke across both of our faces.

"Accomplished!" she exclaimed in a voice uncharacteristically loud, holding the letter with her hand bursting into the air as though jabbing at a cobweb. With that, we began passing the letter to and fro, reading it aloud again and again. At my last turn, I impersonated the voice of my interviewer with all his solemnity and pomp, and my mother began laughing so that the room filled with it.

I was pleased to be telling Papa the news in that very room at the close of the day, and I relied on the echoes of my mother's laughter that remained in order to manage what I imagined would be discontent. However, another surprise was in store, for he was not at all as he usually was in these instances where I had disobeyed him and, with my mother's help, had achieved something. In general, he was one to bellow, as when he found me outside his workshop. Instead, he was silent. He met the news with incredulity and something else I could not recognize.

Just a few months ago, on the day I told him you would come to live with us, I had a similar experience. I expected when I told him the full story of you, he would grow dark and surly as he was known to do. Instead, tears filled his eyes, which was something unfamiliar.

"What is it, Papa?"

"Your *mammina* would have been so happy," he left off without sounding entirely finished.

Tears then sprang to my eyes as I realized my selfishness. I had not considered what it would mean for my mother to come to the end of her life without ever meeting her only grandchild.

We wept together then as the twilight descended and the sitting room grew dark around us. She was gone from both of us, and we finally held the sorrow together as we had not yet been able to do. After a bit, your *nonno* patted the spot next to him on the couch, and I went to sit with him. Not generally an affectionate person, he pulled me to him then, and we sat, finding comfort in sitting together.

Though it was only a few months back, I cannot recall just now how we wound around to the topic of my acceptance to medical school, though I remember the conversation clearly and will attempt to transcribe it for you here.

"I did not believe they would let you in," he told me.

"Why is that?" I asked, with my head still resting on his shoulder.

"That was not the way the world worked, Mimi."

"Did you think the world would not change, Papa?"

"I did not think you would be the one to change it. I did not want you to be the one to change it," he said, looking now at his hands, which had begun to fail him.

This was curious to me, and so I sat up, turned on the nearby lamp, and asked him, "Why not me, Papa?"

The December winds whistled and rattled the windows. "I wanted a tranquil life for you. I wanted to provide you and your mother with every comfort, everything you would need for a happy life so that you would want for nothing. Over time, I came to understand that neither of you wanted that, not because I was offering it, but because you wanted to do it for yourselves. The day you were rejected from medical school, I felt a terrible confirmation that the world was not ready and you could not succeed on your own."

"But then I was accepted," I added.

He nodded at this and said no more; but in that silence, I felt something lay waiting.

"Is there something I do not know?" I asked. He offered another nod, this time with an accompanying shrug.

There was a long stretch of quiet then, and I sat content to wait, but what he told me next was a surprise. He had petitioned the Pope to intercede on my behalf. My acceptance to medical school directly resulted from this.

I tell you this in part, *tesoro*, because it has altered everything I thought I knew about my father; and as you come to live with him, I want you to understand the soft underbelly to be found there like the gastralia of the crocodilians, or the hidden, tender stalk of the porcini.

Even as I write this, I realize that by the time you read it, you may have already learned that on your own. I witnessed the shift in him even in our short time together as a little family, how he dotes upon you as he did my mother. *Nonno* will be your supporter as he has been mine—constant and not without comment!

Now I have to lie down. I hope to discover that this will quell the rising sea within me even if the ship continues to lurch this way and that way. I may resume telling you more tales of medical school following this introduction, though in this state, I may find it difficult to be in the details of that time enough to write it well.

Chapter Five • 1894

Again, the night was the worst of it, and now the winds have subsided. In my dreams, the salty air of Chiaravalle rises, bringing in the loose days at the shore with my mother gathering seaweed to dry on the wooden racks outside the kitchen or hauling in satchels of it to spread upon the gardens. Looking out across the sea in those days, there was a sense of spaciousness lost to me in Rome, which I remember now aboard this ship.

The ship is a hearty vessel, yet beautiful in its way. The thick lengths of rope appeal to me, and I appreciate the care involved in creating the symmetry of the coils, the way the crew loops them inside of one another as concentric circles. Studying them these past days has given me an idea for a new material that perhaps I will try in the Casa in the future.

Watching the crew coil them when trimming the sails sets a hypnosis into motion, coil upon coil, the length of rope growing shorter as the circle grows larger. Of course, the care is less for my pleasure and more for the easy unwinding when it is time to let the sails out again. I was up on deck only once when this happened, and there was a bustle as the ship hands each took a station, then held the end set across the top. In an explosion of motion, they hoisted the sails up, and the lines, guided by the man overseeing the pile, disappeared as wondrously as they appeared, though far more quickly and with no effort. This is something to remember: preparation leads to ease in action. Or preparation over correction, for if you are prepared and do it well, then less time will be spent fixing it.

Much of my time has been spent at this typewriter in my cabin, though the rest of it, when not at meals, I spend outside partly as an antidote for the rocky seas, which I may be getting the hang of now. As a result, I have begun a new relationship with the sky. I do not know if there have been so many days in a row since my days at the convent when I can say that I have really noticed the sky, that I have looked at it with interest and for an extended time, and perhaps I have not considered it at all. This daily ritual is changing me, as I sense I am a different version of myself than when we set out on this voyage. Which returns me to the story, to another time of being altered, a time of needing to move with what was before me in order not to be stopped by it.

On the first day of medical school, at the age of twenty, I entered the building, having dressed and undressed several times that morning. When I arrived, my shoe briefly caught the hem of my skirt, and I faltered at the threshold, which had the men eyeing one another. In that tiny moment, the challenge ahead was evident.

Rollo hung back and put on that we did not know each other, and so I acted in kind, keeping my distance and not seeking him out. We gathered as a group in the long hallway, awaiting the opening remarks.

Medical students from various years were together, and it was clear which were at the beginning as there was a fair bit of shifting from foot to foot, though the new men were greeted and introduced themselves. I stood alone, wrinkling my toes, holding my back straight, watching the pageantry as though invisible to them, thinking of Elizabeth Blackwell in America and how she had completed medical school before I was even born. My mind flitted across the pages of her biography, the image of her determined, dignified face. As I was soothing myself in this way, one gentleman stepped forward to greet me.

"Giuseppe Montesano," he said, and as we shook hands, I remembered meeting him at the Anatomy Lab.

"Maria Montessori," I said in return, hands tingling, taking his gaze frankly, with the sounds of our similar names echoing in the long hall.

He allowed his eyes to stay on mine, and our hands grasped in the act of greeting for a trice longer than customary. It was a small moment yet large in the remembering.

The rest of that first day, first week, first month is a morass of elements that eventually fell into a rhythm, which is mostly what I remember when I think back on medical school. That first year, however, is something I have tucked away and not aired, as it was a difficult time with many obstacles appearing regularly in my path. At the time, I believed it would be the hardest experience I would endure; such is the mind of youth.

I suspect if I were to attend medical school now (a preposterous idea to see appear on paper before me with the ocean bobbing outside a porthole within arm's reach) that it would be a much simpler situation for the ways the world has changed and the ways I myself have changed. However, at the time, determined as I was, there was no softening the experience of being the only woman in the hallway. Though the previous years of schooling had held fewer and fewer girls as the years progressed, I was never the only and by no means the brightest. I had not considered the comfort it had given me until it was gone—such, I think, is true of much in my life. At this juncture, I am making a note to be more aware of what brings me contentment in order to fully appreciate it, however briefly it exists.

One scene that is now bursting forward that I have not held in my mind since is the day they assigned us to the Anatomy Lab. The list went up, holding times when each of us was expected to report to the Lab for ongoing work with cadavers. I approached the board where all my classmates gathered, and I felt an excitement rising to imagine returning to that room I had been in only once but well remembered. I waited patiently for the gentlemen before me to find their names on the list and note their group with what day and time they were expected. Rollo came behind us and began pushing his way to the front of the group, and the smaller men were allowing him through. I held my tongue as my mother had counseled me following a run-in with Rollo that led to some choice words exchanged. "Walk away next time," she told me simply.

"He should walk away," I had insisted. "He is the one who is wrong!"

My mother shook her head, pushing her knuckles into the bread dough, then flipping it over to knead the other side. "Must you be so hot-headed, *mia cara*?" she asked—less a question and more of an invitatation.

The words "hot-headed" rolled around in me after that, and as a result, I was determined to become more aware of my temperature and, thus, more able to control it. When I felt my temperature rise, usually in response to Rollo or a slight from a professor, I would actively work to keep it from rising into my head, breathing, finding my feet, and repeating a word in my mind. The word I used during those years was the name of our old rooster, *Cretino*, which I usually needed during moments with Rollo. I believe he had realized this was the perfect opportunity to make up for the days of our childhood when there was less privilege in his maleness and, thus, we were more fair rivals on the stoop of the apartment. Now, however, circumstances had clearly shifted in his favor, and he held his head high with his chin tilted slightly forward, walking in a way that reminded me of our Chiaravalle rooster.

Perhaps this is asking to be written on these pages as I have only recently learned the English translation for *cretino* on this voyage, and the word has a ring to it that captures my experience of Rollo then: *nitwit*.

At the time, I was only repeating the name of our rooster, *Cretino*. Though I was small in the days of Chiaravalle, I remember clearly waking each morning to walk to the henhouse behind my mother, watching her long skirt catch the dew from the grass. She would first open the hatch that let down the ramp, and the chickens would come out single file. Soon she taught me how to spin the wooden latch that let the door ramp down, and I could manage this on my own while she went for the grain.

I would watch the chickens scratching and moving about, ensuring the world was as they had left it at dusk when they had ambled up the ramp inside for the night. The rooster, *Cretino*, would appear and march around as though in charge, circling the hens and tipping his head back. Soon my mother would return and hand me a small cup of grain that matched her larger one, and we would stand tossing feed to the hungry hens. *Crema* was my favorite. When she hatched, she differed from the other chicks and grew to be beautiful; her white plumage was shinier and fuller than all the others. Sometimes the grain would land on her back, and I would watch closely to see how long each speck would last before sliding through the sleek feathers and landing where another hen would peck it up.

This chicken-tending was a soothing start to each day, and as I grew, I eventually cared for them without my mother so she could attend to other tasks.

It was on a day when I was alone that I noticed the backs of some hens had missing feathers. I described this to my mother and observed in the late afternoon at the second feeding to see if there were more missing, only to discover that now *Crema* also had a spot with feathers gone.

Before running back with the eggs to report to my mother, I decided to hide and watch for myself what was happening to my hens. I tucked myself behind the tall flowers and watched as they pecked up all the grain, then resumed wandering the yard in search of bugs. Soon I watched as *Cretino* lit upon *Crema* and began attacking her back with his beak. *Crema* squawked and tried to get away, but the determined rooster stayed on her.

Before I knew it, I was moving from behind the flowers and after him, waving my arms and chasing him with such a fury that if I had caught him, I might have hurt him.

I burst into the kitchen door, "*Mammina!*"

Our home was a quiet one, and this disturbance roused my mother from her thoughts, and she looked startled, turning to me with a question on her face.

"*Cretino* is attacking the hens!" I was indignant, and my voice rose, calling her to action.

She wiped her hands on her apron and followed me out into the hen yard, inspecting the damage to each of the hens with me following behind her, saying their names and narrating the damage she saw for emphasis. It is a memory that holds the feeling of absolute certainty that my mother would know what to do to fix it. Her mind was preparing to lead to ease in action.

That night we had rooster for dinner.

My father asked, "Are these tomatoes from our garden?" and my mother answered, nodding at me. "Yes, Mimi helped me harvest them along with the basil."

My father chewed slowly, "The sauce tastes like summer." And for a bit, we ate summer, knowing it was coming to an end, until my father asked, "The meat in here is pork? Leftover from the last pig to the butcher?"

My mother shook her head. "No, the meat is fresh."

"There is such gristle," my father responded, nearly on top of my mother's words, and then continued. "Is it just this one piece, or was it not the freshest cut?"

I continued to look at my plate, toying with the bits of basil on the surface of the sauce, and my mother replied, "Definitely not the freshest cut."

I began to laugh then and burst out that it was *Cretino* and that I had helped my mother pluck him. My father excused himself from the table and did not return while my mother and I continued eating until it was all gone.

On the day the Anatomy Lab schedule went up, I held back, repeating *Cretino* in my mind, practicing patience. The other men parted for Rollo, and he turned, spouting about his preferred time in the lab. When he saw me moving towards the list, he made an abrupt turn to look back at it, perhaps to ensure I did not receive his same preferred time block. He stood looking longer than expected, and just as I was approaching the list myself, he turned and crowed, "She is not even on the list. She does not exist!"

The other men were either more polite or not nearly as offended by my presence in medical school, for at that moment, they did not take up

Rollo's stance or even seem to understand it entirely.

I stood reviewing the list methodically from top to bottom, searching for my name or perhaps a misspelling of it. When I reached the bottom and there was only Montesano and no Montessori, I turned abruptly without a word and began down the hall.

This seemed to inflame Rollo, who continued his taunts as my steps echoed down the long, polished hallway.

When I arrived at my professor's door, he had me wait a full hour before admitting me. During that time, I studied the office in great detail, observing the woman who answered his telephone and stored his papers. She was careful not to make eye contact with me and was thus the perfect subject, though I watched her peripherally, for when I watched her openly, her behavior changed as though affected by my gaze.

Finally, I was allowed into the office to speak with the professor.

"What is your concern, *Signorina* Montessori?" he asked without looking up from his papers.

"The Anatomy Lab schedule has been posted without my name included." I had prepared this simple sentence while waiting, to be sure it held no heat.

"Hmmm ..." he uttered as he continued reading.

I stood waiting, not willing to give him the satisfaction of restating my purpose. I was there before him: I did exist.

Some time went by before the woman at the front desk knocked lightly. When he looked up, calling, "Come in," in response, he seemed surprised to see me.

The meek woman peered around the door and announced she was leaving for the day. He nodded and appeared to return to his papers when I cleared my throat.

"*Signorina* Montessori, what are you still doing here?" he asked.

"I am waiting for a response," I said simply, keeping my voice even and my tone matching the woman at the front desk to the best of my ability.

He tilted his head as though considering or deciding before saying, "You shall have to report to the dean on that matter."

"*La ringrazio,*" I responded, thanking him formally, though my head was throbbing with the pressure of my rising aggravation. Without a reply, he returned to his papers.

I repeated nearly this same process with the dean, the chancellor, and the president only to discover that I was ineligible for the Anatomy Lab as it was improper for me to be in the presence of a cadaver in a mixed setting. This took nearly a week to uncover, and by that time, it was just two days until the Lab was to begin.

On a walk to the library with my mother, I shared the complete story, at one point rousing a cluster of pigeons with my fierce gestures and rising tone. My mother nodded and did not quell me, allowing instead for the pigeons and the eyebrows of the passersby to alter my storytelling.

When we arrived at the library steps, she asked me, "What do you want to do next?"

Having sensed this was coming, I had mentally prepared a list that began with aggressive acts of which I am not proud, nor do I remember them as worth repeating. Needless to say, by the time we entered and were greeted by *Sig*. Rapport, I had nearly exhausted myself with sentiment.

"*Saluti*," *Sig*. Rapport said from behind his desk as we entered. He sat more often these days, as his youth was behind him.

My mother must have greeted him in response, but I imagine I was distracted by my dilemma and neglected to do so promptly.

"Enjoy your visit, *Sig.ra* Montessori," he said to my mother. And to me, "*Signorina* Montessori, would you do me the honor of assisting me with a small task before you are off to enjoy your visit?"

It was during that period of stamping and moving books that the idea arose that changed my experience, and to this day, I cannot be sure if it was my idea or his. *Sig*. Rapport had a way of asking questions that led me to understand my own questions and therefore clarified what I needed to do next. On this occasion, his questions led me to understand that all I wanted was to work with cadavers. I did not need to change the policies of the University of Rome Medical School or prove myself to Rollo or the men whose offices I waited in; I merely wanted to learn. Once I came to understand this, it was clear what to do next.

The next day I submitted a written proposal to the President outlining the need for a separate Anatomy Lab for women and citing the University policy about access for all accepted students. I was an accepted student who needed access to an Anatomy Lab, and it was the legal obligation of the University to provide it.

The following day there was a new notice hanging in the long hall indicating the time and location for an Anatomy Lab with one enrolled participant listed below. Thus, I began my Anatomy Lab in a lightly renovated basement storage room beginning at eight o'clock in the evening.

I felt the victory of this throughout my entire body and ignored my mother's concerns about the location, time of day, and isolation. Instead, I walked boldly to the school after the sun went down, only to find it dark and locked. This was an initial disappointment that only fueled my determination. After that, each day that followed, I remained in the building for the full day in order to be there past closing. My mother packed a hamper holding a supper that I enjoyed in the long hallway before descending to the basement.

That first night stands out in my mind; when the ship creaks, I can hear again the strange noises of the school building echoing through the passageways of the basement as I descended to begin my learning.

I will tell you that I very much enjoyed the process of seeing the inner workings of the human body, how our own rigging loops and coils. The most fascinating of all was the brain. To explore the pathways and see how it is organized to fit perfectly within the cranium was a revelation and learning I continue to return to. For though it was at first intimidating and admittedly at times alarming to be alone in the cavernous, rumbling basement of the medical school, it was also entirely freeing. I was left alone without interruption to explore for as long as I liked the areas that intrigued me. This, I think, would not have been my experience were I to have been sharing a lab with Rollo and the other medical students, and so it is with gratitude that I look back on this time of independence and free exploration.

If I were to name events in life that shaped me and my work, *mio caro*, I would name this near the top of the list. It encompassed all the elements, being both a significant challenge—to continue long days and push myself to descend into the darkness of the bottom floor with only a dead person as company—and also significant satisfaction with a new world open to me as a result of doing just that. I wonder what will be ahead in your life that will prove to be such a worthy challenge? You have so much of your life stretching out before you with so many choices.

This turns my mind to a conversation early on in our voyage on the ship as I was sitting on the ship's deck with a group of wealthy travelers. One among them was a gentleman from Milan who studied as an attorney but was now in business. This fact arose as the party was joined by another gentleman, currently practicing law, who mentioned having attended the University of Bologna, which prompted the businessman's wife to report that her husband had attended that very same program. The attorney immediately became nostalgic, asking about what years and sections, but the businessman hesitated. He clearly did not enjoy the discussion of professors and the traditions of the University, and I was intrigued by this.

"Where did you go to clerk?" Attorney asked Business.

Business cleared his throat. Attorney's face shifted ever so slightly, and being unable to endure the wait, he tossed out places, naturally starting with his own, which he felt to be most prominent, and moving down the list from there, waiting for agreement.

The rest of the group began shifting in their deck chairs as we could all feel the inside of Business in a way it seemed Attorney was immune to. I wondered then how Attorney managed in a courtroom so oblivious to other people, and I concluded that perhaps it made him even sharper and able to be ruthless in his questioning as he seemed unaffected by the situation of others.

When Attorney got to the bottom of his list without Business having claimed one, he determined that Business had moved out of the area, and he waited for agreement on this conclusion. Unable to bear it another moment, the wife of Business, who I will call Pluck, breaking social norms, inserted herself into the men's conversation by announcing, "He went into business."

That evening, I found myself seated with Business and Pluck for dinner.

"Have you enjoyed being in business?" I asked. I had leaned forward enough, looking at Business, to clearly indicate that the question was directed to him. However, he did not pause from eating.

"*Amore*," Pluck prompted him, and I sensed she may have touched him with her foot beneath the table, for his body lurched, spilling some soup from his spoon.

Feeling an upsurge of mercy for this man, I repeated myself without request.

For the rest of the dinner, I was thoroughly engaged in the conversation as Business revealed his story to me. It happened gradually, his reluctance waning as I asked more and more questions about his life choices, and he came to piece the tale together as though he were understanding it himself for the first time. He had fallen in love with Pluck, who was from a wealthy family in Milan, and he had left Bologna to return to Milan and become part of her father's business. They had three grown children, of whom they were both very proud, glowing as they talked about them and their first grandchild, who they hoped would wait to be born until their return from America.

"How does law school fit into your story?" I asked him as dessert arrived.

The trust had grown between us, and so he was able to tolerate the directness of my question and, in fact, appeared to appreciate it.

"I have regrets," he began. Pluck turned to look at him with a revealing swiftness. "That I did not leave the University when we first met," he inserted quickly. They held eye contact, and I looked at my dessert. "Had I left sooner, I would not have incurred the debt your father repaid on my behalf, and I might have come into our marriage on more equal terms," he said directly to his wife.

"Had you done that, we would not have had the children we have, for to change one thing is to change everything," Pluck said to him so tenderly that I needed to strain to hear her over the surrounding conversations.

This scene from the ship is to share with you how much this idea moves around in me, slopping on the sides of my mind with the rocking of the boat. To change one thing is to change everything.

Like Business, I elected to study something I did not directly pursue. Unlike Business, I regularly appreciate the many ways that experience prepared me for the next piece of work and continues to inform my thinking. Without those years in medical school, I would not have had the knowledge, the skills, or the insight to have done the work in education that brings me now to America. This is something to keep in mind as you make your steps into the world—it is not important to know your path's destination and to walk directly there, but rather to be willing to follow it as it is laid out for you. Our society does not encourage this, *mio caro*. You must decide for yourself.

I will tell you now that through the hardening experience of medical school, I became a bit egotistical. I did not realize it at the time, though had I been more receptive to my mother's suggested modifications, I might have grown less so. Such is the prerogative of youth, however, and so I launched into the world thinking I could do anything and that I was entirely unstoppable. My hubris of that time pains me now to remember and to admit to you as you are just coming to know me, but it is the truth, and that is what these pages growing under the ship's paperweight are being written to tell. I will not deny my own arrogance or reshape it into something more palatable, for it is an essential piece of your story; and in that, I refuse to deny you anything, despite the cost to me now.

When the long road of medical school was completed, I had a brief period of unrest. I recall the first day following the culmination ceremony and how restless my legs felt without their familiar destination. I had fallen into a routine that, once my mind was set on it, I was able to do regularly without fatigue. This involved rising early and working into the night every day, with the exception of Sunday, which my mother had planned in our usual way.

The day it was all done, and there was nothing to rise for, was a dull day indeed. I have since read the wisdom of pausing and resting; however, as I look back over my life so far, I see that I have not taken naturally to it. Even now, as I am on this luxury ship making its way to America with all the comforts one could want, I have plunged into this project as though resting would blunt my edges.

Without much delay, however, the University of Rome hired me to be an assistant physician in their Psychiatry program. It was not the surgical position I believed I wanted at the time, and I moped about, despondent that, of course, they had placed the only female in work regarding feelings.

My mother would not tolerate moping of any kind and promptly put me to work after hours restoring the woodwork on our dining room table.

"Your attention to yourself is not flattering, *mia cara*," she said quietly one evening as we were first stripping the wood.

This stung, and I had no words, burying my face in the side of my arm as I pressed the planer into the wood of the table. "How was it she could not see what I was up against?" I thought self-righteously, internally defending my situation and thinking my mother terribly wrong without saying a single word aloud.

Now I wish she were alive for me to admit my conceit and to grant how unbearable I must have been during that time. And even as I type that, I can hear her laugh and see her face as she allows the confession without needing it. She would not be vindicated in the least, only perhaps a bit pleased in my ability to acknowledge it.

Chapter Six • 1898

When I drew the cabin desk drawer open just now in search of more sheets to roll into this majestic machine that stays with me through it all, even as I thump it with my palm in utter consternation, I found this written in French on a small scroll of paper: "*Divide each difficulty into as many parts as is feasible and necessary to resolve it.*" This accurately captures my feeling about both the tale I am stumbling to tell and also about the typewriter key that jams so that the letter *t* repeats—*ttttt*— imitating the fluttering of flags outside my porthole as we turn into a gale. I sense a rise in the rocking, both inside and out. So, coming upon this corrective notion of dividing difficulty is both timely and critical to keep me moving in the story. Confusion acts like wrong coordinates on the spinning navigational equipment. This was a view I have had, and yet as we come to know each other, I can only feel blessed with the repeated opportunities to alter the difficulties and perhaps even resolve them. I will then take the advice and divide the difficulty of telling the next segment into the parts necessary.

With that, I will tell you about the romance that ensued coming out of my first medical post. There are three crumpled pages on the floor of the cabin that hold a rather autobiographical version of this where I report how my interests shifted and were piqued by various elements of the work and the men doing it, but they have been pulled out of the stuttering machine and discarded for good reason. The typewriter sensed I was prevaricating and consumed each one with the letter *t* until I found my fortitude to come out with the ttttruth.

When I was appointed to direct a school, a new institution called the Orthophrenic School, in Rome, Giuseppe Ferruccio Montesano was my co-director. I have mentioned him in this script already, and so you are aware that we shared a year in medical school. He graduated ahead of me and had, in fact, advocated for me to be called to the position, without which it is doubtful they would have appointed a woman to such a post. It would be a joy to report that I was selected on merit—because I was, after all, at the top of my graduating class–but we had overlapped in that first year of medical school. We had not forgotten each other.

Dr. Montessano had returned once a year in order to act as an examiner for the graduating class, who were facing a final review prior to graduation. Each time we saw each other, there was electricity, much like what is in the air on the ship just now as the lightning flashes seem to strike the roiling sea.

Perhaps this is an overly dramatic description, yet I had not experienced such a feeling up until that time, and it overtook me. It held a similar charge to the rising anger I felt towards Rollo, yet on the pleasant end, and it was a feeling that seemed immune to my re-centering strategies. I became flustered and clumsy, often flushing and knocking into things, once toppling an entire medical cart with all the sterile instruments tumbling and scattering down the hall, the echo of which caused other interns and doctors to poke their heads from doors to witness the catastrophe. Nurses clucked their tongues and shooed me, as I once did the chickens, to ward off my clumsy attempt to assist in righting the upset.

On those occasions, should I catch the eye of Dr. Montesano, I would see his great delight, as though he enjoyed the circus of events that often surrounded me when I was struck in his presence. This experience of being flustered in his presence was countered by the other meetings we occasionally had when he would appear at the philosophical lecture series, and we would sit for at least an hour past the end of it to hotly debate the meaning and mind of the speaker. Perhaps in hindsight he held no particular point of view on these, yet he came to know mine by always arguing to the contrary, inciting me to a point of great passion on whatever the topic might have been. It was these conversations that led me to understand my own position as I reasoned from one angle and then the next, both inspired by his attention and also gratified by the experience of understanding my opinions as I spoke them. The supposition that speaking ideas could be a point of origin rather than a point of arrival was a new one. It allowed me to understand that my way of talking through new concepts could be seen as a strength rather than something to conceal.

And so, on the day I received the letter appointing me as his co-director, it was with a hot-air balloon's expanse that I called out to my mother, and nothing short of a miracle that my feet stayed on the ground as I ran with hands tingling, flapping the paper, into my father's study to report this turn of events. The feeling as I held that letter, which I have kept for you, *mio caro*, was that my life was about to change. It was as real and sure as knowing when you are about to yawn or that it is about to rain; it's a smell, a flush of feeling through you.

Thus began the time of seeing Dr. Montesano every day, working so that our elbows nearly touched, and our rhythms of living fell in sync. Each day I was up before first light, writing notes of what I had thought of since my eyes closed and dressing hastily to begin the day together. I flew about the house, breezing past my mother, who admonished me for skipping over breakfast and holding out a lunch pail I barely paid attention to in the day, often bringing it home to her unopened. I grew thin with the thrill of the work and his company as we grew closer daily.

I just now went into the details of that work and how it prepared me for the work I am called to do now, yet the typewriter seems to notice when I digress and has eaten that page entirely. I am left to keep to the facts that pertain only to you, though if I may slip in one thought here— the study of different children, those who struggled to fit into Italian schools, in this medical-pedagogical institute where I trained teachers to think differently, has much to do with this story, enough anyway that the typewriter has not rejected this one sentence.

Dr. Montesano and I grew closer through this work and the success we were having at the Institute. We began dining together, not with cold bread and cheese at the office, but out in the world of *ristorantes*. Had I been more clear-headed during that period, it might have occurred to me that he was then engaging in courting behavior. He carefully chose where we would dine, and they were exclusively places with lit candles, linen napkins, and proper place settings—as though we would need all of those utensils in the same meal!

Of course, I remained focused on his mind, and all that bubbled up in mine as a result of a single sentence from his. Our dialog was a tapestry of topics—all passionately discussed with a fervor I now understand as a precursor to what we would soon uncover. An insulated sprawl of thought and feeling, an island untouched, unseen, unheard by the rest of the world, so that a nomenclature of our own making emerged holding us as a hammock might a ragged sailor.

And all the while, there were these intimate moments, gestures, indications of what was to come—our skin touching in ways that acted as bellows to the fire within me.

We were a closed circuit, just at the outset of uncovering all that lay between us, when his mother came for a visit. An elegant woman, she strode into the Orthophrenic School with her dress bustling about her, and the commanding nature of her struck me nearly dumb. Dr. Montesano greeted her somewhat cautiously, it seemed to me, with her extending her hand to him, as one would do with an acquaintance. She then held his shoulders firmly beneath her gloved hands and stared directly into his eyes, stopping him from any further movement.

"You look well," she determined after a moment of silence. She tipped her head curtly and released him.

He faltered then. The shock of it flashed through me to see that. I had never seen him falter. Falter, waver, vacillate—even back to our first meeting in the Anatomy Lab with a room full of uncertain peers, he had stepped forward cordially and with great steadiness. Through all of our dinners and the fluid transition to being together in other, more physical ways, he was even, determined, intent, and resolute, as though it were the most natural thing in the world. Seeing him falter then was jarring.

It was in this disrupted state that I first met your grandmother, *Signora* Isabella Schiavone Montesano. She approached me next as I had seen farmers in Chiaravalle approach a cow they were considering taking home as their own. Inadvertently, I shook my head to ward off this association, and to bring myself back into the room. My toes wrinkled, and my back straightened under her gaze, with my chin extended farther than necessary to compensate for the bovine reference lingering. Perhaps this is what drew her to place her fingers under my chin, tilting it this way and that. From farm animal to marionette in one gesture, and the anger began to rise in my face.

Dr. Montesano was by then adept at reading my weather, and he stepped forward hastily with a formal introduction that led to clasping fingers in the feminine version of a handshake. To my horror (and my mother's great amusement when I recounted this scene), my knees dipped then of their own accord in the first and last curtsy of my life.

At that moment, *Signora* Montesano insisted on including me in a dinner at a lavish establishment I had then only heard of but never visited. I considered the invitation, looking to Dr. Montesano to see his reaction, and our eyes held, causing a flutter in me as I recalled the previous evening, his hand exploring the skin on my forearm. His eyes said, "Please," and so I agreed.

Back at our home, my mother ironed as I moved my hair about upon my head in hopes of creating an elegant appearance. She laughed lightly as I described this first encounter, and the tinkling of the laughter uplifted me. I saw in the looking glass my own serious nature peering back, the look of one who has been intruded upon, put out, and so I worked to soften the expression on my face, the tight grasp in my chest. My parents had yet to meet Dr. Montesano, and this was the first of family introductions. It stood to reason I would feel unsettled, yet I need not submerge into such a negative position.

Behind me, across the room, I watched my mother's capable motions as she smoothed the wrinkles from my dress, carefully pressing the hem so that it held its shape well when she raised it from the board. Her gentle nature lay juxtaposed with that of *Signora* Montesano.

"Perhaps you could come?" I suggested.

My mother let loose a small laugh before she saw my face. "You are serious, *mia cara*?"

Unnecessary tears emerged from the corner of my eyes, and I looked away from the looking glass and the nest of hair I had pinned above.

She crossed over to me then and placed her arms around me from behind, saying, "*Carissima*." And that was all it took before I had turned and thrust myself into her.

"She is cold and harsh, and I am filled with uncharitable thoughts ..." I sobbed into her warm body.

My mother caressed my hair, unpinning it, and when I quieted, she pulled back and began to redesign the faulty architecture that had been my coif. "What would you like to do next?" she asked.

I took air into my lungs so that my chest rose and watched the creases of her face as she concentrated on her work of reorganization. "Truthfully, I would like to impress her," I said quietly. I was not proud of this sentiment, for it did not live within my belief system for one to seek to impress, and it also startled me to see clearly my romantic feelings for Montesano in light of his mother's gaze upon us. I was a buffet of feelings and knew not my own mind.

"Of course you do, *mia cara*; that is only natural." More pinning and then a hand on my cheek, "And you know you are already impressive— there is nothing more you must do. The hardest part will be not to get in your own way tonight."

I cast this idea over myself as one would a veil, determined to hold it through the entire experience, from the outset to the close of the evening. Whatever occurred, I would not be separated from myself.

This turned out to be fortunate indeed, for I was tested from the outset. *Signora* Montesano talked for much of the journey to the restaurant of her ancestry, tracing it to the House of Aragon, the rulers of southern Italy. The tilt of her head as she offered the lineage seemed a practiced one, and my eyes moved to evaluate her son's response to this pageantry. He evaded me, showing serious interest in the weave of his trousers, and soon we had arrived and were entering the establishment.

I understand now that *Signora* Montesano's intention that evening was to evaluate my suitability and that before we had even taken our seats, she had determined me to be unbefitting. I wince a bit, envisioning what unfolded from this perspective, yet I will forge ahead and reveal it to you so that you might understand my early guilelessness. Pretensions have always confounded me, and I am deeply grateful to the Accardi family for the earnestness they have instilled in you. It seems you may have been spared this sort of critical condescension as part of your inheritance.

"Tell me of your parents, Maria," *Signora* Montesano said, smoothing out her burgundy velvet dress skirts as she settled into her seat.

"They are at home, likely enjoying this cool evening." I smiled at her and made a similar gesture towards my skirts, though it was more to occupy my anxious hands than to prevent wrinkling of the fabric. Fortunately, it brought to mind the image of my mother with the black iron held aloft, and I felt my shoulders relax and the slightest upturn in the corners of my mouth.

My eyes returned to the conversation in time to see *Signora* Montesano look directly at her son as though jabbing him with a hot poker.

He turned his eyes to mine and smiled while telling his mother that my father was Alessandro Montessori, an accountant in the civil service, and my mother, Renilde Stoppani, was well-educated with a passion for reading.

At the time, I missed entirely that this is what she had been asking me—to report in return the story of my ancestry. Instead, it pleased me immensely to hear Montesano describe my mother in this way, and I beamed at him. At the sight of this, his mother became quite cross, knocking the water glass over as she gestured to him to stop talking. The water cascaded across the table, flowing over the edge and filling the lap of my skirt so that when I looked down, there was a small pond forming. Surprising us all, I did not jump up but instead sat, considering what I might do next.

At this point, Montesano's mother turned to him and dismissed me. "Send her home," she commanded as she disappeared behind the menu.

My mouth began to form words in response when Montesano's finger landed gently on my lips in a gesture of earlier intimacy. This single admission of our deeper connection had the effect of stilling me, and I turned my gaze from her to him. With that, I felt his grasp upon my elbow, and he was guiding me to stand, causing the water to land upon my shoes, filling the right one so that as I walked to the door of the establishment, holding my head high, I perceived the slightest slosh.

I must pause here as the wind hurls the ship from side to side and a loud crack reverberates. Up until the crack, I have much enjoyed that the outside environment has been rightly mirroring the tale I have been just now unraveling. From the point of realizing I was under review, the shaking and shuddering of the vessel intensified—right up to the spilling of the water and squeaking of the shoes. Now, however, I am beginning to believe it is possible that I will die at sea with my fingers on the keys telling you this; and if so, then may it be so. Let the story end here.

●

There has been a long pause with the length of this page spooling out of the machine as it slid from side to side on the desk, almost taunting me as I lay ill in the cabin, unable to manage the immense rising and falling of the vessel. I focused on your face for a good long while, and that helped me to remain steady longer than I thought possible until the moment when all resistance was defeated.

Through the emptying of my body, with the ship cast asunder, the spirit of my mother came to me, and I felt her hands upon my shoulders in a soft, most loving version of her find-your-feet gesture. She remained with me through the darkest part of the night, a solace to me as always, until finally, I slept, waking in the late afternoon to find the storm had passed and the rough seas were soothed by the light of day.

As my eyes opened to blue, there was such a collage of feelings that I quite understand why Mr. Picasso and Mr. Braque have begun this recent practice. A mix of images—the heavy, black iron, the rich burgundy dress, hands holding and waving dismissively, a hairpin, a leaking shoe, a rueful glance, and a doting one. I lay quite transfixed by the power of casting all of this onto paper, the blur of that scene in my seasickness, how it summoned my mother to me when I most needed her, and soon I was weeping again at the loss of her. She has died in advance of her time, and I do not agree. I recognize that even if I do not agree, I must begin to accept this truth; and still, I do not yet feel ready.

Eventually, I was lulled by watching the paper flap from the roll of the typewriter. Earlier, I had cranked open the portal a bit to freshen the atmosphere, and our story ruffled in the air moving about the cabin. Though I was not yet quite ready to return to writing, it prompted me to make my way out onto the deck into the fresh air. There were very few people there, and yet it felt as though we had weathered something together, and all were amiable with the relief of it, your mother most especially, as it was a relief to be outside of my own mind for a bit of time.

I suppose the weather arose in order to break down the difficulty into smaller sections—bringing us back to the French scroll that I found blown into a corner upon my return and have just now secured with the paperweight: "*Divide each difficulty into as many parts as is feasible and necessary to resolve it.*"

Now, while the unpleasantness is still fresh, I shall reveal to you the stormiest part of this tale in order to resolve it: my reflections on illusions of triumph. This is the part where I leaped when perhaps I should have stepped, where I threw the sails of my heart up the line when perhaps I should have held the rigging tight. I see now it was a custom where I came from—how I had always lived—and a privilege that would be stripped from me.

A history of pure exuberance landed me in the arms of Montesano in spite of the fact that his mother had forbidden him to marry me. In her mind, women were to focus on lace-making and the study of music, and my refusal to acquiesce to those terms meant a firm and clear decision that her noble son and I were not to be together. Writing the word *noble* prompts me to understand from this vantage point that I did not come from a pedigree of her preferred caliber; the Montessoris were a station beneath, and the mixing would weaken the Montesano bloodline.

And yet we were as drawn to one another as sea swells are drawn to the hull of this ship. The force between us was overpowering, and her forbiddance created the perfect conditions- the thrill and intrigue of such a rebellion. As a person who values my liberty, my freedom to choose, his mother's belief that she could choose on my behalf when even my own mother understood this was not possible ignited a defiance in me that I soon regretted.

Already I had broken every rule society placed on me as a woman, but being physically intimate outside of marriage was beyond reason. The result of that intimacy was an unwed conception. I faltered then, and the shock of this new reality caused me to retreat. My mother, who had been my advocate at every turn and championed choice after choice that flew in the face of convention, did not deserve what would certainly be societal condemnation. And my papa, who had the cultural power to stop me, had not done so. He had silently funded and otherwise supported every decision I had made. By that point in my career, I had begun to travel, speak, and publish nationally and internationally about the children at the school and the methods we had discovered. Their success had drawn interest and attention, and I was aware that my situation would not go unnoticed. This was not to fall on my parents, so at the height of my career, I left Rome abruptly.

Leaving Rome with you at the start of gestation and not yet publicly noticeable meant leaving my parents for the first time in my life, a choice I made without fully appreciating its impact. Having always held a daily cadence with them, it was foreign and disorienting to be separate. I see now from this distance how leaving may have added to the disorientation, where at the time, I was not aware of this element as I rumbled with the abrupt change in my life.

My destination may surprise you. I ended up in the Franciscan convent on Via Giusti in Rome. I entered with the blessing and protection of the Mother Superior, who allowed me a bed in the cloisters and simple garb that suggested I was a novitiate but which kept me out of conversations with the long-standing nuns in residence there.

I mopped floors. I worked in the garden. I read texts for the Mother Superior, whose eyes no longer worked as she would like by the day's end with the light dimming. I arrived in September and stayed through the winter into late spring, watching the seasons come and go as a long contemplation. I polished the crosses in the sanctuary, marveling at the craftsmanship involved in many of them and feeling the burn on my face as my expanding front brushed the largest one that hung at the front on the altar.

I see now that I had been dismissed, *mio caro*. I was dismissed first by his mother, and then, once I was pregnant with you, by Montesano himself, who suggested I retreat until the "moment" had passed. I left Rome in a swirl of conflicting thoughts and feelings, with some hope of returning to the work and love with Montesano.

You knew nothing of this. You grew in me each day as I swept and weeded and scrubbed. You grew in the peaceful environs of the Franciscan convent while the seasons shifted around us, while my heart spun out, perhaps understanding what my head resisted: that I was at the end of something fast expiring, like the German *wunderkerzen* throwing sparks in all directions until the gunpowder has burnt down and then you are left holding a simple wire coated in iron and nothing more.

My interest during those months was held by the two small children of the kitchen extern. Before attending to my other regular duties, I was set to report to the kitchen each morning first thing for preparations, peeling potatoes, and such. The kitchen extern, Angelina, would arrive with her baby and toddler, one in each arm. Though I was there to work, I found my attention drawn by the habits of the small children. Up until then, I had only studied children who had been institutionalized and presented unusually, so it fascinated me to watch these two round-cheeked children, one trailing her mother about the convent kitchen and the other either tied onto his mother's front behind her apron or stashed in a crate nested with oat sacks. Perhaps my circumstances had me alert to human life at its origin and early unfolding, for I watched the baby intently, noting his changes from day to day. He developed before my very eyes and gave me a sense of what was to come as I continued to churn the choices around and around in my head.

I had already concluded that I would not terminate the pregnancy. For whatever other customs I flew in the face of, I was not immune to the views on the sacrament of life—and in truth, from the outset, it did feel sacred. It was as though I knew the moment you took root in me, and from there, I was in freefall to discover what to do next.

I had not spoken of my condition in a forthright way with the Mother Superior, and yet she did not remark as my dress size grew nor when my ankles swelled to the size of those of a dainty rhino. Perhaps her failing eyesight contributed to the situation, though it was not my intention to conceal what was happening, only to be spared conversation on the matter. Fortunately, in the convent, I conversed with no one outside of Mother Superior and Angelina.

As the time lengthened, I felt the choices in my head as chicken wings flapping when startled from roosting. There was the idea that we would return together to Rome, causing undue scandal for my parents. Or that we would go somewhere else together, breaking out of the community I had worked to form and leaving my professional life behind as well as your father. Or that I would deliver you and leave you off at hospital to be raised by a family who had lost a child of their own.

None of the options felt to be the right ones. As I worked to acquire a friendly feeling towards them, I was unable to do so. It neither felt right to clutch you to me nor to entirely give you up.

I carry with me always a letter my mother sent me during that time, and I will insert it here in this missive. Perhaps I will use this as a place to collect the fractals of my story; the component parts, if found on their own, might not reveal the fullness of what they reveal together. This is how I have begun to understand the human mind's making of mathematics in an era when teaching each piece separately seems highly valued. Why would the overall intersectionality of the component parts of mathematics be wittthheld from children until they are old enough not to care anymore?

But the machine reminds me, I digress again from the tale I am here to tttell, and I will put that thought into another book. For now, I am putting down the idea of compiling the individual elements into this document as a sort of archive for you to inherit when you want to understand the breadth of the story. Your *nonno* gave me the sweetest collection of newspaper clippings over a dozen years ago, for my thirtieth birthday. When I return from America, I shall add it here as well.

My mother's letter:

Mia Cara,

You have been gone for only a few weeks, yet the time stretches out as endless without you in residence to perplex me on a regular basis. There has not been a single sewing needle found stuck into a napkin or a swatch of drapery, and it is possible I have begun to lose my skill for searching out these treasures, these small signs of you and your breakneck approach to all that you do, without time to properly stow the very tool that crafted your product. I fear I have contributed to your haphazard ways by not having properly instructed you on this when you were small. As a result, all is lost, and what once caused me great consternation is now the very thing I miss in your absence.

In your last letter, you remarked that you have not been feeling well of late, and I hope that has passed by the time this reaches you. If you are to be away, I like to think of you as at your most robust. Perhaps one of the nuns has provided you with a tonic that will serve to stabilize and fortify. If not, I would encourage you to ask after such wisdom.

At the heart of this letter, Mimi, I want to make clear my position on your current situation. You may think that I am unaware of your feelings for Sig. *Montesano and the choices you made regarding those feelings, but I must assure you that a mother's knowing reaches far beyond what she is told. This, I sense, you will be discovering for yourself within the next months and then years. The umbilical cord you were so intrigued with in medical school connects you to the person you are just now creating and will continue to connect you in spite of what the world has to say about it.*

There has been no greater use of my life than to watch you grow into the woman you continue to become, and I fervently pray that you will elect to allow this privilege once again when you are ready. Regardless of the circumstances, your home remains your home.

Now that I have gotten that down, I will report to you that your papa has been in quite the mood these past weeks. We have not spoken of your situation, so I have no firm evidence, though I sense he also knows what has transpired. He paces in the sitting room at reading time as though he cannot settle. He moved your chair three times until I was finally prompted to admonish him to let it be. Letting it be is not in his mental construct, and he looked at me with his head tilted like one of the chickens when they would see me approach with any bucket and not offer the contents to them. Perhaps that is what you are doing now at the convent—seeking to let it be? If not, I invite both you and your papa to consider it as an option. We are all still interconnected, having lost nothing, and, for the time being, perhaps we reconcile ourselves to the way it is now.

Amore, Mammina

It was this letter that spoke to the crisis of faith I was quietly nursing across those lonely weeks of gestation. It was this letter that opened in me the space to accept what had happened and move into what needed to happen next. And this letter, from the heart and mind of my mother, I tucked into my most precious belongings—those I carry with me wherever I go.

Though I still did not see the way through and did not understand the best decision, I did see that chasing the answer only exhausted without result, and I did understand the power of my mother's suggestion to let it be. To be with what was. To live in the moment and trust that the answer would reveal itself.

You were born on March 31, 1898, healthy and alert, at the dawn of the day. I have not seen a more beautiful sight than your face looking up at me with such familiarity and resolve.

There is no reason not to say it: you undid me. Your sincerity from the outset, your knowing eyes trained on me, your small fingers looped around the tip of my smallest finger, creating the illusion that it was enormous—that I was a giant. I was daunted by the unwanted power I held as a being who outsized you so entirely.

I began to pray. I confess that my faith had been intermittent and that, as a scientist, I had given less attention to the church and the ways of religion. It was a familiar ritual, but not one that I had invested myself in particularly. Religion, with its steadiness, had played a role and fulfilled me with its regularity and its impact on my parents, which is to say it soothed them, and thus I was soothed.

Now in this context, this place of worship, this holy place, following months of dusting statues, I was opened to the point of feeling the full force of spirit. I wept with the power of it, the way it held me when I felt so utterly alone.

If truth is what novitiates are seeking, then I understood a new truth, a union, or an interconnection with everything around me. Your arrival in this world had opened my aperture, and I was seeing, smelling, tasting, hearing, and feeling that which had been previously muted or less detectable. I had spent my early adult years in various aspects of acceleration with little attention to meandering, stillness, or reflection. Now you brought me to a halt, and I fell through the hole in time where days passed with little or nothing actually accomplished, but rather everything noted and absorbed through the newness of your experience. Had the morning bells chimed as sweetly all along, and I was just now awakening to their music? I recall them only as a prompt, like a doorbell asking you to open the door or the jingle of the elevator announcing arrival at your chosen floor. I had arrived at my chosen floor, and those weeks were a time of appreciating sustained transcendence, God's hand on the back of my head.

It took me eight weeks to be ready to leave the convent, and I spent that time exclusively in the kitchen with Angelina, her babies, and you. My more regular time there began on a day early after your arrival, when I grew restless within my chamber and tested my steadiness with a visit to the garden. Mother Superior was on a bench there with her head tilted towards the sun, and Sister Thomas sat nearby mending, acknowledging my arrival with a nod before returning her attention to the stitching. Mother Superior, however, beckoned for me to approach. We had not spoken since the day we discussed arrangements for your impending birth, and I felt shy and exposed as I approached her.

"You look remarkably well, Maria," she said, looking directly into my eyes, as was her way. "And I am pleased to see you outside so soon." She did not turn her eyes to you nor acknowledge you there in my arms.

My mind chased a proper response, and finding none, I nodded and offered a half smile of gratitude.

"How is your strength?" she asked.

I tilted my head from side to side to indicate it was fair and widened my smile a fraction.

"Ahhh, yes," she said and nodded sagely. "Perhaps a cup of Angelina's tea is what is needed now." She suggested this to the trees behind my head, looking past me and continuing to bob her head slightly in agreement with herself.

When I arrived in the kitchen, Angelina had the kettle whistling as though she were expecting me. She poured me a brew with an aroma that drew me from the withdrawn place I had retreated to, and when I inquired after its name, she began to talk with me, which in the previous months we had been hesitant to do.

At first it was about the herbs, their origins and medicinal purposes, but soon she shared stories of her life growing up. Her childhood was spent in a small village outside of Rome, and her family did much with the bit of land there, including harvesting a special blend of herbs for a tea so compelling that I was drawn back to the kitchen for a cup each day without fail, coaxing her to tell me more about her home and spending an increasing amount of time in her company. Her descriptions brought me back to Chiaravalle, and I would ask her endless questions about the details of life in her own village. Soon into these conversations, I began to feel something unknown to me where the past, the present, and the future began to blend into one vision, collapsing into one reality. In my dreams, I would see you as myself toddling about the kitchen garden, chasing the hens, and watching birds flit across the open sky. When this blend of time occurred, whether awake or asleep, I was not in the vision—neither the mother weeding nor the child chasing—it was only you I could see there.

Such was the expanse of time when no decision needed to be made, only holding a hot cup of tea, drawing in the earthy smell, walking the grounds with you tucked in close to me, and suspending the usual propulsion forward.

Six weeks following your birth, Mother Superior called me to her chambers for the first time. This was unexpected, and I thought perhaps I had overstayed my welcome there and that, without knowing my next move, she was about to ask me to depart.

I arrived alone, having left you in Angelina's care in the kitchen, nestled sleeping in a potato crate filled with soft oat sacks. I knocked lightly on the door. When there was no appreciable answer, I rapped harder. Still, there was no word from the other side of the wooden door, and so after a third try, I pushed the door gently and peered into her chambers. She sat in her day chair with her head bent to one side, and I saw right away that her eyes were closed. I stood on the threshold debating as I wished to avoid startling her and, at the same time, not certain how long you would stay asleep in the oat sacks.

I cleared my throat. Nothing happened. I crossed the threshold considering heavy steps, but my feet would not make them as it seemed entirely lacking in grace and courtesy to stomp toward a sleeping person, never mind a sleeping Mother Superior! Outside the window, the sky was breaking into light through a thin spot in the thickness of the April clouds. The sun came across the floor so suddenly it was as though a spotlight had been turned upon me, and in addition, upon Mother Superior.

This shift in brightness caused her to stir, and at that moment, a second clearing of the throat proved effective. She raised her head to consider me standing before her with my hands clasped at my front.

"You look quite unsure, child; what is it?" she asked with a slight rustiness in her voice following her rest.

"I was told you wanted to see me?" I replied.

"Indeed, that is true." She lifted herself in stature, and in doing so, her small bible slid to the floor. Though her eyes were no longer able to make out the words on the page, she continued to carry this reminder of the words that seemed to travel in her head most of the time.

I stepped forward, fetched the book, and placed it wordlessly back into its position on her lap. She nodded and resumed talking.

"You are on the precipice of departure from us, are you not?" Her eyebrows lifted as she asked this.

"I am," I replied simply.

"You have been in discernment, yes?" she paused, and I nodded in reply. "And has your heart not been wrestling with indecision?" She asked this in her direct, yet indirect, manner.

"It has," I replied.

"And what conclusion have you reached?"

As I recall this dialogue, I am struck by the discretion and kindness in her line of questioning, though at the time, I was only aware of how her questions allowed me to follow her into the conversation without feeling forced. This quality has made it into what I shall be speaking about in America, but I am onto myself now about these digressions from your true story, and so I shall delay writing more about that until another time.

I recall the afternoon light upon my shoes as I considered them, hoping words would form to answer her question. She was patient and sat without shifting through the long silence that followed until my eyes rose to meet hers and she saw that I had not reached a conclusion at all.

"Ahh ..." she murmured insightfully, picking up her book reflexively and rotating it in her hands as though it were a billiard ball rather than a bible. When she launched into talking, I realized she had been holding back, respecting whatever I had decided; and now with the clarity that no decision had been reached, she brought her idea forward at such a pace as I had not experienced with Mother Superior.

"There is a small village nearby with a family that would be well-positioned to care for another child. They live on a healthy piece of land with fresh air, fresh food, and much care for one another. They are not a staunchly religious family, yet they hold the word of God in their every action, and one would be privileged to grow up there. This is not to say they are a family of such means as yours, yet their wealth is felt upon entering their cottage. I have only had the opportunity to visit one time, and yet it made a lasting impression upon me, and I often wonder what I may have been capable of were I to have grown surrounded by such goodness."

At that, Mother Superior seemed to become momentarily lost in thought, her eyes drifting to the window, her face taking on an unreadable expression.

"Would you be so kind as to crank open the window just a bit?" she asked after the extended quiet. "I know Sister Thomas would scold me if she saw it, but if we remember to close it before you leave, then perhaps it will be a pleasure reserved for this moment alone."

When I had done as she had wished and returned to stand before her, she was then ready to deliver the remainder of her thought.

"What would you think of Mario entering into the care of this family?"

My hands began to tingle. In spite of the fact that I had understood her suggestion in the course of her description, I found myself stung by the boldness of her sentence as though she had reached up and struck me in the chest with her bible. At the same time, it felt as if my own mother's hands had just landed on each of my shoulders in her find-your-feet gesture.

To avoid stammering, I said nothing, allowing my heart to return to a more typical pace. She held my gaze throughout this process.

As my heart steadied, it also softened, and my mind began to picture you in the scene she had described. An enmeshment of nightly dreams and daily stories in the kitchen combined and landed in the world she was offering. In doing so, my expression must have loosened ever so slightly, for she responded to the shift.

"You have become comfortable with Angelina?" And in her asking, I then understood her suggestion in its full form.

From there, *mio caro*, all the rest of it fell into place, and you and I left the convent at dusk two weeks later with Angelina to join the Accardi family on their farm.

I stayed with her loving family for the three days following before I departed for Rome to reenter the world I had left.

Having already spent a good deal of time with her children, Stella and Luca, in the convent kitchen, I noticed they adjusted easily to finding me in their own kitchen. Angelina also carried on as though it were the most natural progression without cause for disruption or the

need to become ill-at-ease with one another. All of this goodwill transferred readily to her husband, Lorenzo, who was most gracious with me
throughout those three days and beyond.

Perhaps the notable, unspoken piece that rises up for me now in
the retelling was the difference in our stations and the way that held
us apart, even in the kitchen stirring porridge or turning the sausage.
I was an educated medical doctor from a known family in Rome. My
privilage traveled with me to the Accardi's farm kitchen as an identity
inseparable from the hands that prepared the breakfast. While I was
most grateful over the course of those days that my mother had prepared me to engage in every task, to prove myself useful and capable,
there was a gap, nonetheless.

On the second morning, Lorenzo came upon me cleaning out the
chickens' water trough, scrubbing it down severely with a set of tree
needles, as I had been taught. It was not immediately apparent to me
that he was there, as I was deep in the satisfaction of the task. When
I caught the movement of his trousers in the wind, I peered up at him
from where I knelt, and the look on his face brought me to my feet.

"*Buongiorno, Dottoressa,*" he said quietly, and with those two words,
I understood that an act most natural for me (and perhaps most satisfying after all the cleaning of clean crosses at the convent) was disturbing
my host in a way he was too courteous to put words to. Without ever
articulating it, even to myself, I adjusted my behavior accordingly, and
we passed the remaining days with greater ease.

On the morning of my departure, we cooked an especially large breakfast, adding sheep's cheese and early greens to the fresh eggs. We set up the meal outside in the spring sunshine on the wooden table in the side yard and sat for a time afterward, watching as Stella picked the small violets from the grass and Luca crawled about sitting from time to time to gnaw on a stick or leaf he had come upon. We laughed at the expressions on his face as he sampled what the earth had to offer. Inside the comfort we had created was the awareness of the significant change ahead, and I held you in my arms, though you were sleeping and could have been rightly placed in the basket.

In the quiet of the morning, before we rose to clear, before we set the departure into motion, Lorenzo spoke. "We will take care, *Dottoressa*," he said simply, his voice low and steady. With those few words, my tears fell upon your head. I was leaving you to grow up with the Accardi family; I would not raise you on my own.

In my discussions with Montesano, he had made it clear that he was not ready to be part of a family. As I write those words, I am aware of how he hid from what may have been the bigger truth; he was not willing to stand by me, by us. The work at the Orthophrenic School was meeting with such success, and public attention may have dimmed had there been a scandal revealed regarding the true nature of our relationship and the unsanctioned arrival of you. The word he used was "private." He was more comfortable keeping our love private. He asserted that I was his one love and that we would remain wed in our hearts, in a spiritual union that would last throughout our lives. I took these words as truth, and they lured me back to Rome.

My weeks then revolved around work as a doctor in the city with regular visits to the countryside to see you grow plump and happy in life there. Your first year moved with such alacrity that I allowed myself to dwell in the liminal space of possibilities—you were neither given up for adoption nor were you in the public eye as I gained notoriety. Surprisingly, I had no doubts at the time but rather fell into it as a most natural rhythm.

And what of my own hiding, now glaring under the watchful thump of the typewriter keys? Did I hide the truth from myself as well? That by holding two worlds, one in the city with Montesano and one in the country with you, I was hoping to keep both? When ultimately, it meant I ended up with neither.

If this all seems a convenient retelling of a decision you find reprehensible, then I would very much welcome the opportunity to appreciate your point of view. As we have come to know one another these past months, we have not yet broached the topic of my choice nor had the occasion to discuss it. Perhaps by the time you read this collection of pages, we will have already done so. If not, then you may read this as a direct invitation to approach me at a time you are ready to explore this subject. There is much I want to know about the days and weeks I missed, the internal life you cultivated at the cottage, the stories you created in your own mind about how it was you were growing up without your parents at your side each day.

As I look out onto the vast ocean, now somewhat calm in the afternoon sun, the words that want to be written next are a reminder that to change one thing is to change everything. May we reconcile the choices of the past in the context of who we are as a result of them, rather than carrying them as regrets that weigh us down like cannon balls. We are now free to make our own story. May that lighten us, add an air current to help us rise.

Chapter Seven • 1900

Rocking has become the new way I experience time and space, and I wonder if I shall arrive in America and be unable to stop. Perhaps I shall be standing in front of a collected audience and my moving stature will be so compelling that they will begin to sway with me from side to side, as one does reflexively when standing with a mother holding her infant. In some ways, this captures what I hope to begin in North America—the collective attention of some in education who may wish to sway towards this new way of working with young children.

Now and then, I hear a bell, as though a character in a play were having a realization, and it just chimed again. During the day, the music of the ship travels so that I can hear the violin and piano almost all the time.

Out on the deck this morning, in the early quiet before the instruments were lifted for the day, I watched the captain when he believed he was alone. He strolled along the upper deck with his hands linked behind him, his shoulders back, and his chin up, a posture implying his satisfaction with the voyage thus far. He kept his gaze out across the sea, and the look upon his face was one of great gratitude. This is surely the look of one who has found his right vocation and is living it with fulfillment.

The next part of our story is where I myself fell into step with my right vocation.

As I mentioned, my return to Rome was punctuated with trips out to the cottage to visit you in the care of the Accardis. They were kind in their welcome, always ushering me in and seating me in the nicest chair, the one with stuffed arms to rest upon, the faded fabric covered with roses.

In your first years, I observed you without drawing your attention. You were secure in your connection to Angelina and Lorenzo and spent much of your time watching and absorbing the world around you. You walked easily. Though I was not there to see it occur, Angelina sent a message for me to come when I could. I was away on a speaking engagement; so by the time I arrived, you were chasing after the chickens in a full-throttle monster walk. We sat outside and laughed, watching you lift your legs and drop them, as though they were imbued with great power and we should expect the ground to shake upon impact!

Such focus and concentration on your face in those early days and how naturally you took to learning and language. I have books full of notes taken while watching you learn from your environment and, by two, you had many words to attach to them. Perhaps one day, I will share the notes with you, though you may find my script difficult to interpret as they were not meant to be read by others but rather recordings for my own remembering.

There was a predictable unfolding of each visit to the farm, which often began with a visit with Lorenzo.

"*Dottoressa*," Lorenzo addressed me formally from the start. "How is your health this day?" And then we would continue on to exchange pleasantries regarding the health of the household and the happenings in the time that had passed between visits.

Angelina would emerge from the kitchen with a child in her arms or on her hip, sometimes both, and greet me warmly, kissing me on both my cheeks, a gesture I rarely participated in outside of their home and my parents'. She would slide you into my arms then, as naturally as if we were back in the convent kitchen and she was handing you back after holding you while I completed some task. Angelina no longer worked at the convent now with three children too old to bring along to work in the kitchen, and so she had often baked or made something that was part of the visit.

On a day three years into these visits, Angelina greeted me with you trailing her. As I sat down, she went back into the kitchen, but you stayed. Lorenzo fell into a new tale of the farm - the fields, the harvest, or maybe it was about the livestock. I admit that I was following it all only loosely for the distraction of you, noting all the ways you had grown and changed, as you fingered a button on your shirt, working to push it through the hole. It was as Lorenzo began hypothesizing about a pair of rabbits that I picked up the thread of what he was saying.

"Most believe only a small number of animals mate for life, but you should see these two—ask Angelina—they are never separate. We see them all over the land together. I believe they are devoted …"

I did not hear the end of his thought properly, though, as I was over-come and began suddenly to weep. He stammered and came to an unceremonious end, which offered me the opening to retreat to the kitchen. You followed and watched as I leaned heavily against the wall, crying into my hands.

Angelina approached when I entered and then allowed me a long moment, saying nothing. She neither advanced nor retreated, standing solidly on two feet, waiting. The blurping of the soup on the stove was the only sound in the room, though I could hear footsteps of the other children upstairs and the turning of the windmill in the distance.

"Montesano is engaged," I told her, my voice a hollow metal box.

She considered this.

It may not surprise you to know that Angelina was the one person who knew that your father had refused to marry me as a result of his mother's displeasure with the match. He had attempted to soften this by giving you his name and agreeing never to marry. He had skillfully activated my rebellious nature by claiming marriage as a convention beneath us that was not worthy or necessary, given the richness of our love. I believed him. I believed our love was beyond all bounds and would continue on in spite of his mother's beliefs, in spite of the separateness of our family.

This is the story I had believed. This is the story I told Angelina. She had never spoken one way or the other on the matter, accepting my acceptance. She kindly expanded her family to include you as a way to support that narrative, never offering her opinion or speaking her doubt.

Now the account felt to be fiction. Now the façade was revealed as just that—a pretense, sham, hoax, ruse, deception. I stood before her leaking with remorse, and at that very moment, I understood it to be something she had seen all along. She recognized that he would not be true to me or join me in this experience of being changed by you. He then found another and, not only that, had proposed marriage to her. The betrayal was acrid, lacerating, astringent. The humiliation utter and complete.

Neither of us spoke; even once the torrent ended, we remained quiet, you still at my side. As I calmed, I felt your small hand upon my skirts and wondered how long it had been resting there.

Slowly, my mind turned to the usual question it held in these types of moments. "What do you want to do next?" In that space, you turned to consider me, eyes black rings around a universe.

I heard a voice in my head then. It was an answer to the question that came not from my own mind but from outside of me while still hearing it from the inside.

And so, this was the day I announced that I would not go forward in the life I had known before your coming. The declaration surprised me as I had not known just how much I was enduring rather than enjoying each day. Yet when I opened my mouth and spoke, when I heard the words, they were stated as a fact, as certain as though I had announced it would be dusk soon.

"I am leaving medicine."

Now the ship is pitching a bit, and I am aware of the way the ocean narrates the feelings of this story so accurately. It was an unexpected truth that emerged for me that day in the kitchen where you grew up eating your meals. Both Angelina and I knew its power and impact on my life as I said it, and yet with her hand caressing the top of your head, it was also clear that she understood the source of the shift. Your arrival was an utterly remarkable occurrence that was invisible in the world in which I worked, and yet I was forever changed and could not continue on as though nothing had happened. The move your father made to declare his intentions to another had shattered an illusion I was living in and, in doing so, prompted me to declare my own intentions.

Angelina turned and prepared tea, which we took outside to sit on the bench in the late afternoon light. The children joined us. Stella ran about the yard chasing butterflies while you and Luca played at our feet. We sat without talking and only stirred when the chickens began to roost.

Fortunately, my mind did not race about, thrashing as it sometimes does, following my proclamation, but instead, I slipped into a state that I have experienced only a few times in my life so far. In that state, the immediate demands of life fall away, and I am suspended in time in a place very near God. I tell you this not from a stance of importance, but so that you will know the layers of one of your creators. It is a manner in which I find my way and one which has not disappointed.

When we stood up in the dim light, I knew the next steps I needed to take, and the path was as clear as lamplight showing the way on a summer night's stroll.

I returned to Rome and resigned from my prestigious post as the co-director of the Orthophrenic School, where I had worked those past years. I had a short, frank conversation with Montesano, letting him know that, in fact, you would not take his name after all. In addition to leaving medicine, I was also officially ending our association. I will not share the details of that conversation, but I do hope that as a man you will hold less arrogance when it comes to women, and you will perceive yourself as an equal partner rather than the dominant one. I believe you will be more fulfilled this way, but also you will be living within the truth.

This last conversation your father and I ever had was revealing to me in many ways and instructive regarding my own hubris and un-willingness to see what was evident. My inability to see what was right before me was based almost entirely on my inflated view of myself. The reflection of myself in his self-centered manner and entitlement was sharp and piercing, inviting a course correction.

What was needed next was time for introspection. There appeared two options for this time of reflection: to do it at home under the steady guidance of my parents or to return to the convent. In many ways, it was a very simple, even obvious decision, as I very much needed to sort it through on my own in the kind of quiet expanse offered me during your gestation. My family had offered such comfort in my life, and I was in a time of dearly needing the familiar; yet since I had not been entirely forthcoming about you, there was a tension, a dis-ease. The unspoken, in a household used to speaking, lay below the surface like a fault line.

For the three previous years, we had resisted; we had struggled; we had buried. We did this and more to not say what was real and true after a life of speaking directly. My mother began one cleaning project after another, including one that had all the curtains off their rods, scrubbed thin with the unspoken, and then hung in long swatches of "I wish, could we, what if" that caught the air entering the windows she had thrown open. She then took to the windows with newspaper and vinegar. Our house had never been more immaculate.

We shifted, we wielded, we worked, but we did not unbraid the thoughts that had raveled together since I returned from the convent after you were born.

Such anguish crossed my mother's face the day I returned without you. It stays with me, and I feel what I have felt many times now in telling you this story, a sheltered grief that I am slowly pulling into the light. As the blinders that were there fall away, I see with greater clarity the impact of my solo decision—on her, and yes, *mio caro*, on you.

The part I wish not to set down in words anywhere, no less to you with a typing machine that shouts it out with each click of the keys, is where I hurt her. Beyond the cruel act of returning alone, without a word about my choice, without a wavering or a tear, without explanation about my trips to the country, there was what I finally did with my words.

I have no excuse, Mario. There is nothing she ever did that caused me to lash out in this way; nothing in her countenance that deserved it. She was a sure and steady part of my every day, and I pushed her away in my desolation.

I would like to say that, at the time, the only antidote I could find was to keep moving. If I stayed in motion, there was an order, a sense of purpose that allowed the confusion to abate. Taking the house apart with my mother made complete sense at the time, and we both benefited from the industry.

If she had only left me to it—as she once had with my tile scrubbing—I might not have pounced upon her so. And yet, that is perhaps a quiet sliding into blaming the one who did nothing wrong. She loved me and wanted me to have the life I wanted. She silently accepted my choice. It was I who caused the row, who lashed out instead of taking refuge.

It was the day following my resignation and my final conversation with Montesano, and we had just taken the carpet out onto the balcony to beat it. We thrust the heavy weight over the empty flower box, and birds scattered across the piazza. I took the broom and began thrashing the dusty rug so that particles flew in all directions. My arms stiffened, and I went after it with a vengeance, all the bound-up rage finding a home in the beating. The humiliation of Montesano's engagement was a fresh wound that I protected in every way, and when she remarked upon the violence of my actions, somehow insinuating I may have been thinking of him or that my anger was misplaced, I turned that very emotion upon her.

"You know nothing of it!" I shouted. "You know nothing of him or of me! You live a sheltered life of reading and knitting with no idea of the pressures I face, the life I am trying to live. You know nothing!" I threw the broom with such force that it flew off the balcony, landing with a clatter on the stones below. In the stunned silence that followed, I turned and fled, leaving my mother alone on the balcony in the aftershock.

I have not shared that moment with anyone. Perhaps the lowest moment of my life.

Following that, I elected to take a retreat at the convent, and my parents were in support of this decision. I had torn something with my mother that I left unrepaired as I departed to tend to my wounded heart and pride and to chart my next course.

Being back at the convent allowed me to spend much time walking about in a state of reflection upon all that had occurred and my own role in its making. Thus, I emerged more aware of my fallibility and the potential impact of my headstrong nature. In short, I discovered humility, perhaps for the first time. If, at first, it was uncomfortable as I considered it, I began to feel it growing on me. I no longer expected myself to have the answer to everything, and this was liberating.

There was just now a tinkle of bells from the deck, and as I looked out the porthole, I saw the astonishing sky with the light waning and the colors pouring in from all sides. Or I suppose, more rightly, the color is pouring out as it is emanating from the sinking sun. Interesting how the mind can invert that, though it knows quite properly which direction the light moves from.

I look back at these last pages and see that I have glossed over the crux of it. Perhaps this is a call for me to be more forthright with what I have just written here, to acknowledge that there was brokenness at that time. And to tell you that I was suffering, though I have never dwelt on that aspect and think it is not wise to do so here either. There was simply something in the thought about the sun's decline resulting in an array of colors that led me to want to tell you that, indeed, during that time, I felt as though my sun had set. Losing the ones you love is a grief like no other. Through all the disappointments that preceded that time, all the hardships, some of which I have written to you about on these very pages, I had never been so cut through to my center as compared to the loss of the imagined life with the two of you. And in addition, I had created a rift with the one who loved me unconditionally.

I observed an argument in my heart during those days. To have loved Montesano so fiercely and blindly and to have ended with nothing, my hands empty, was a complexity I continued to turn over. To have loved unabashedly with the core of my being and to have thought myself met in that devotion, only to find myself utterly alone, was a bit like the aftershock of a devastating earthquake, one that brings down your personal city to absolute rubble.

At the time of your conception, I had imagined such a different story unfolding that I remained astounded, walking alone through the grounds of the convent at dawn. How could it be that I had been treated so finely, cared for so well, listened to, encouraged, and supported, and that love was now entirely gone? Not only had I lost such a love, but all of what I had was now promised to another. I had believed it was unique—that I was a person to him like no other—and to have been summarily replaced was a blow I struggled to tolerate.

My heart disputed the truth, and my head grew weary of going over it again and again. There was simply nothing my head could say that would help my heart to grasp and accept the situation. Without my mother there to sort it through with, this went on for days creating, in fact, a larger tangle of emotions as I grew angry with myself for the toil and then disgusted with my dedication to one who had not earned it nor lived up to it. I stormed around the grounds in the afternoon, dragging a rake across the lawn until my head pounded and my hands blistered. I looked down at my palms and finally saw evidence of the pain I could not escape, which only activated the rage and sent me raking harder at the innocent grass.

My agitation extended into the nights, taking the place of sleep and setting me to pace within my small room until I was like a caged animal that must be set free. I would go then to the chapel where the candles were always burning, and I would ask for relief from this state of suffering, this constant quarrel that would not be quelled.

With Angelina no longer working at the convent, there was a hole. Even my one place of former solace, the kitchen, held only hard reminders of what I had given up, the illusion, the chimera of having a life together ultimately including you, and I could not bring myself to go there. As a result, I spoke to no one.

I must have begun to neglect my appearance as the looks at mealtimes became unbearable. Though meals were always held in silence and nothing was ever said, I stopped going and found I was not bothered by not eating. It made no difference to me either way as I was preoccupied with the inner conflict—who I thought I was and who I now saw myself as being—those difficult days when it was irreconcilable.

The reckoning happened as a result of Grace.

I was alone in the yard, following one of my early walks, sitting on the stone bench there. Mud clung to the sides of my shoes, and my hands were cold as I clasped them together, blister to blister. Something about my chapped and neglected hands brought tears into my eyes, and I spontaneously tilted my head back to the sky, where the colors were soft from the emergence of the day, and asked, "Please help me."

It was not a premeditated question, and therefore I had no expectation that there would be an answer. The clouds were of the large and puffy variety, and I watched them gathering into one cluster. I continued to watch, now somewhat transfixed by their flexible nature, by their willingness to change. I watched over time as they separated and dispersed into the day until it was as though they had never been there at all—the sky as clear and blue as the satin cloth upon the altar.

This is the first time I have ever put words to this experience. That I have tacked it down on the page, like the splayed limbs of a frog undergoing dissection, has lessened the profound nature of the moment. And yet, what happened in the sky that day was finally a story that made sense to my heart—one of allowing change. Not making change but cooperating with the current conditions. Much like my mother's counsel years earlier to "let it be," I had found beauty in the idea of absolute cooperation with what is.

In that moment of understanding, I resolved to reinvent myself. I understood for the first time: it was not predetermined that shifting from a life of medicine meant withdrawing and severing all connections to the work that had so inspired me. In fact, I had the better part of my life before me and could study anything I chose. The relief was tremendous, and I wept there on the hard bench, feeling that I had been given my life back again. The passion I had felt for your father, for the vision of our life together, was not inexorably entwined with the whole of who I was and would ever be. I was overcome with gratitude for this new understanding.

When I left the convent, I enrolled in the University of Rome and took courses in anthropology, educational philosophy, and experimental psychology. I was on a quest now for my life's work, and though I had begun down one path, I no longer held it as a failure to change course. Changing course may, in fact, be critical to the proper navigation of a voyage.

I mentioned observing the captain this morning and his confident stance at the helm. He read the sky and the waves, and I imagine these informed his decisions once he entered the bridge to consult with the navigational instruments there. All of this likely consolidated to form the instructions he would give the helmsman steering our vessel. Likewise, with a human voyage through life, I have found the need to consult multiple forms of data in order to make timely course corrections. These may not be understood by others, those watching from outside you, but they coalesce to form the basis of a life well lived, *mio caro*. That is, after all, what we are here for—a life well lived.

Chapter Eight • 1906

The ship's paperweight died today after a long fight to keep these pages in order. It was loyal and true to the end when it slid off the desk and smashed to smithereens on my cabin floor in a dramatic departure. May it rest in peace. Its job has been temporarily filled by my shoe, though I suspect I will need to reclaim it as footwear before too long. For now, though, it appears quite fancy perched upon the papers on the desk, and it is even possible I caught it admiring the view out the porthole.

Out the porthole, I see the sun has broken through again, and soon I will leave you to attend a meeting organized by Mr. McClure. He has created quite a following for me aboard this ship, which helps to offset the unsettledness I carry having left you again. To be writing this full tale of how it came to be that we lived separately while we are separate does not escape my notice. I think perhaps this will be the last voyage I will take without you. At fifteen, you are old enough to travel, and the world will need to know the boy Montessori. Through your name, if nothing else, you are to inherit what was created next in the tale, the development of the Montessori Method.

I will not now tell you of things you could read in the writings that already exist—both mine and others—of how the method began. Instead,

I shall recall to you the interruption in our routine.

The time spent visiting you through your early years, when you were not so aware of me, changed after your sixth birthday. It led me to understand that humans do not develop only in one way and that there are stages or planes of development.

As you crossed into what I soon came to call the second plane of development, I noticed new characteristics arising. Some of the old awareness or sensitivities you used to have appeared to have dissipated. I became curious about this and asked *Sig*. Rapport to show me the child development section of the library, and though he never asked me outright, it was as though he had a sense of what fueled me during those days. His kindness was endless, and, in fact, it was he who connected me to the San Lorenzo housing authority when they were at their wit's end.

"Have you heard of the situation in San Lorenzo?" he asked as I was checking out a hefty number of books.

My head was abuzz from what I had just been reading in one of the books in the stack to be borrowed, and my hands were itching to grab it back off the counter and continue reading while he labored through his slow process of stamping and recording. "No…" I responded without really listening.

Uncharacteristically, he let a book land harder than necessary on the counter, and the sound of it brought me back into the conversation. I looked up at him. "San Lorenzo?"

A slight smile crossed his wrinkled face as he now had my attention. "Yes, they are building in the area there. However, it seems the young children find the construction most interesting. When their older brothers and sisters go off to school, and they are on their own, they have taken to following the workers about and getting into all sorts of situations. I just learned yesterday from the supervisor who lives in my building that there is one young fellow who stepped on a nail, and it went straight through his small foot."

Perhaps this was an exaggeration of sorts, but it certainly worked to increase my investment in the conversation. I nodded for him to go on.

"I said to him, 'Antonio, what you need is someone to step in and gather those children up so you can get your work done,' and he bobbed his head in agreement."

My hands began to tingle.

The conversation continued from there, and by the time I had loaded the books into my satchel, *Sig*. Rapport and I had imagined the future, and I left with Antonio's information in my pocket. I was soon to be appointed by the Italian government to head up a state-supported school in the San Lorenzo quarter of Rome with sixty children from three to six years old.

I realize that I could go on and on about the project in great detail as it unfolded, and yet it is not the account I have set out to record. It is already in a book for you to read should you want to know more about how this method came to be and how I came to be sailing across the sea to share it in America, and so I will leave it as a silhouette. The outlines are there for you to see—my work at the Orthophrenic School; my study of anthropology, psychology, and human development; and my fascination with your own development—with the rest available as needed.

What is true is that I neglected you during that time.

The words land harshly on the page, and I rolled the wheel of the typewriter to allow them proper space in my efforts not to hide the truth. I am not proud of it, nor am I ashamed—it is simply a truth we both lived and must reconcile between us. I state it boldly here to open the topic with you, as I wonder what you made of our arrangement in those years.

"Our arrangement in those years." I reread that sentence and see that even in this present-day writing, I shy away from taking responsibility—phrasing it as though it were mutually ours, as though I came to it in agreement with you or anyone. When, in truth, the decision was solely my own. I consulted not even my mother on my course of action. Though we moved past our dispute upon my return from the convent, a shift had occurred that began with my first vist. We both understood without having discussed it. I was now making autonomous decisions, no longer in collaboration.

Perhaps overdue in my maturation, and perhaps healthy in many ways, and yet I continue to feel the loss that came with that choice. My mother did not get to experience being a *nonna*, even second-hand, as I told her nothing of you or the arrangement I had made with the Accardis. Thus, when it came time to make a change, I had effectively removed her as a person who might offer me support, stranding myself as an island.

This thought propels me to share what I recall of the day just before your seventh birthday. I wonder how it connects to your own memories of that day, if you have any.

I stood outside the door to the cottage for a long time before entering, as I knew there would be something different about the day. The Accardis had invited me to visit on a Sunday prior to the usual time, and this had never happened before.

The sky was bright around me, brighter than I felt, with a strong, stiff wind boxing my cheeks. The cowbells tolled in the background, and I wondered why there were animals out in the field in winter, even with such sun offering its warmth. My hand moved to knock on the door and then did not, as at that moment it opened.

"You are here!" Lorenzo greeted me with a smile. The light entered the dark house in a seam across his face, continuing into the room behind him. "We have made a fresh pot of tea and some biscuits for your visit, *Dottoressa*."

My feet shuffled across the threshold and onto the thick boards of the keeping room floor. I took off my coat and reached to take off my hat, feeling the stiff black lace surrounding it, and was struck with the sudden urge to hide it in its ostentatiousness.

You approached then. I thought to take my hat, but instead, you handed me a dark rock with white streaks running through it. You had a way of giving me gifts each time I visited, and I felt my cheeks grow red that I had neglected to bring you anything.

The moment passed as Lorenzo hung my coat and hat on a peg, and Angelina entered with the biscuits, the smell filling the entire room with a buttery warmth that prompted my mouth to water. She kissed each of my cheeks and asked after my well-being.

Lorenzo gestured for me to sit in my usual place—the upholstered chair with the roses. Each time I sat in it, I saw Angelina rocking you there when you were an infant and reading to you there as a toddler, and I imagined how proud you were the day you first climbed into it on your own. I pictured your serene face waiting for Angelina or Lorenzo to enter the room and find you seated there, tucked flush up against the back, your legs stretched out before you, matching the length of the seat cushion. Visions of you there, in moments I was not there, always filled me as I settled in, and on that day, I saw you reading the book of Greek mythology I had sent earlier in the month. Your fingers were holding the gold cover, your teeth pressing your bottom lip in response to a gripping part of the tale.

"How was your journey?" Angelina asked, breaking the spell and placing the biscuits on the low table, where I then saw the fruit and plates, the teapot, and cups. Her slender hand reached for the teapot and began to pour. As she set the pot down, she immediately proceeded to fill the small plates with the treasures laid out—the centerpiece: warm biscuits coated in honey, likely the result of the fall harvest from their hives.

What an extraordinary person, I thought, stroking the rock in my hand, feeling the slight ridges of the stripes running through it.

Unbidden came lines from a Giosue Carducci poem: "The sun again arises in my soul/ With all life's holiest ideals renewed/ And multiplied, the while each thought becomes/ A harmony and every sense a song."

"Lovely," I whispered, my eyes suddenly smarting.

We sat for a bit then in quiet conversation, enjoying the tastes and smells. You barely ate, nibbling around the edge of your biscuit and letting your tea grow cold.

"Mario, collect some fresh eggs for the *Dottoressa*, will you?" Lorenzo directed, and without hesitation you obeyed, leaving us to the warmth and quiet of the room. Then Lorenzo turned his gaze to me, and I could see a shadow there that set a skip in my heart. There was something difficult he intended to tell me.

"More tea?" Angelina asked softly as she held out the teapot in my direction.

I extended my mismatched cup and saucer, and she refilled it. The tea flowed dark from the spout, and when it was full, I drew it towards me slowly so as not to spill and also to allow for an extra moment to pass before I was to learn the source of the shadow.

Lorenzo cleared his throat as though to speak, but then did not. Angelina moved in, seamlessly handing me the ceramic pitcher of cream. "We have had many questions from Mario about your visits and want to speak with you about it," she said, looking me right in the eye in her way that was direct without being confrontational.

I received the cream and the news together and held them both without comment. This was the day. All along, I knew the day would come when we would need to help you understand the situation, and now the day was here.

"We have told him that you delivered him."

The cup rattled in its saucer, and the half-eaten biscuit slid off the plate onto my lap. I looked down at it sitting there, honey-side shining up at me, thinking it lovely nested there. I am unsure how long I spent looking at my biscuit before returning my gaze to Angelina and Lorenzo.

They sat together on the settee, holding their own cups and waiting patiently for my recovery. I noticed Lorenzo's left hand was on Angelina's back as though bracing her and thought it remarkable that I had never seen them touching before or even this proximate.

Angelina brought her eyes from the tea to mine. "He assumed that meant you were the doctor, and we have not corrected him."

Lorenzo leaned in as if to speak, but then, noting the slightest movement of Angelina's head, said nothing.

At that moment, we heard the kitchen door open and the sound of your feet entering—customarily scraping your shoes on the rim of the doorway and then taking them off. I imagined you lining them up carefully on the mat there as I had seen you do many times when Angelina and I had taken tea in the kitchen, her stirring a large pot of something for supper, one child or another coming in for a drink or to deliver an egg.

I wondered then where Stella and Luca had been the whole time of my visit, and anticipating my question as though following my thoughts, Angelina said, "The children are with *Nonna* today. Mario was going also, but changed his mind when he heard you were coming."

In the act of moving my biscuit back onto the plate, you appeared before me with a dozen eggs placed carefully into the carton and tied with a ribbon made out of hay, a few dried flowers tucked in where the bow would be. It was perhaps one of the loveliest arrangements I had seen, and my eyes pricked again. I raised my gaze to your face, and you were smiling in such a way that, without planning, my mouth smiled back. Eyes now shining and with what may have been an overripe smile, I opened my arms to you, and you came into them.

"Thank you," I said into your hair.

The front door then blew open, and the room was alive with Stella waving a picture poster of some kind for all to see and Luca blowing on a pennywhistle, followed by their grandmother shaking her head as though she could not account for their excitement. She came right to you and held out her hand. You put your empty hand open beneath her full one, and she placed into it a wooden top carefully carved and painted red with a handle striped in yellow. I watched your face change in delight, and you handed me the eggs before throwing your arms around her and thanking her over and over.

She looked over the roof of your head, where she had put her hand as you hugged her, to me, and our eyes met for just an instant. Just enough so that I knew she understood the conversation we were having, and, in that flash, I knew what was expected. It was time to cease these self-centered intrusions and leave this family to be a family.

"Enough, enough," she said in rough tenderness that was well understood. "All of you settle down. We have trampled in on the quiet tea. Wash your hands up if you would like a biscuit. I will put on the kettle." And with that, she disappeared into the kitchen.

For a moment, my mind followed her out of the room, and again I saw your shoes lined up carefully by the back door, the wood bucket on one side and the egg basket on the other. I wanted to linger in my mind's picture as the match was struck, the stove lit, and the water pumped into the kettle. Yet I knew if I stayed in the kitchen in my mind that I would lose the nerve or the moment would pass in the room where I was sitting.

"Mario," I said, placing the eggs on the table and catching your elbow. "Thank you for the rock and the eggs, such lovely gifts." I turned and directed the next part to the room. "I wanted to tell all of you that I have been asked to begin a new project, and I will not be able to visit as much for a while."

Luca paused for the briefest moment from experimenting with the force of his breath on the pennywhistle before resuming, now trying out different hole coverings. Stella also had a momentary interruption in her movements that passed even before I could turn my gaze to Lorenzo and Angelina on the settee.

Lorenzo was sitting back now, sipping his tea in an ordinary way that misaligned with the ringing in my ears, which had begun at the point of my announcement. He nodded slightly, and Angelina slid back next to him, watching you. She was always such a sensitive and loving observer, tracking you children from a distance with grace.

I continued to watch her face to see a reflection of your reaction, as though looking directly was too dangerous—like looking into the sun.

Yet when you touched my arm, I could no longer resist. Your eyes were soft, your long black lashes blinking, and you left your hand there without speaking. Luca and Stella quieted again as though an extension of you. The room settled into the recognition of parting. We were holding the moment prior to parting so that we heard the clock ticking, the wind on the shutters, and the far-off lowing of the cows. We stayed connected in this way until your *nonna* returned from the kitchen for the teapot to refill with the now hot water from the stove.

"*Mani*," she said to Stella and Luca, breaking the stillness and sending the room back into motion as they left to wash up for biscuits and tea.

When I left that late afternoon, I had decided to stay away from you for a stretch, to let you live the wonderful life you seemed to be having without further intrusion and disruption. Angelina held me in an extra-long embrace as I prepared to leave. I wanted somehow to capture that moment in order to revisit it during the weeks and months ahead. I took it in through my nostrils—the scent of breezes in her hair, soap flakes in her dress, soft remnants of biscuits in the background.

Perhaps this is why I remember it all so clearly, though it has been more than half your life ago now. The sharpest part of the memory, though, is the way the door clicked behind me. It was nearly dark, and the light was pouring out of the little windows. You on the inside. Me on the outside.

Looking at the sky, I asked for one thing to hold on to, and when I opened my hand, I found your rock; your beautiful smooth stone had been there all along.

So, you see from one side how we came to be apart as you moved from the first plane of development into the second plane. Perhaps for my method to be born, I had to leave you in full for a time.

Looking back, I can understand with my mind what my heart knew all along, and yet to answer to what the heart knows to be right is not always the easiest task. Perhaps people will tell you to allow your heart to guide you, as though that is easy; but I must tell you, *mio caro*, it is, in fact, most difficult. It is as though to be blindfolded and asked to find your way home through the woods—an act of faith and courage. To believe in guidance beyond what is known, to be led along a path you cannot see. This is the kind of faith a true life must be built upon, for we do not have all the answers to life's questions. It is our task to follow the guidance offered by responding to what is put in our path, to negotiate the obstacles without fully understanding.

I certainly did not understand at the front of the work I have done what would become of it. I blundered into the arrangement in San Lorenzo and scrambled to create a setting for learning, but none of it unfolded as I might have laid it out in a plan. That is the miraculous part to appreciate—that had I planned it all out from my mind rather than following my observations and my instincts, I would likely have created something entirely different and likely not nearly as effective.

As I said, the government commissioned me to begin the school in the San Lorenzo quarter as a way to contain sixty small children, and you cannot imagine all that I learned in that first year, Mario. I made more mistakes than I can report to you here, and yet each one led me to a greater understanding of what was needed. Having been raised with friendliness towards error, I did not shy away but rather pushed into each new learning.

I had previously worked only with those impaired in learning, and yet I found much of what I had developed to work quite well with young learners. What I had not anticipated was how very secure the children would be in operating things once I had given them instructions. From there, I thought how much more efficient it would be to speak with them as a group, as I had observed in the other nurseries, but in fact, I found that practice quite useless. It seemed what they most desired was a prepared environment with real activities to occupy their hands. It seemed the most effective way was to offer them the instruction individually, with few words. In fact, many of my early presentations to the youngest in the group were ones I did completely silently, looking at them and then at the point of interest with an expression to reflect my own absorption. When I allowed my eyes to slide over to the child, they, too, had the very same expression of absorption and curiosity.

Another of my early discoveries was attempting to use the furniture that had been delivered to the apartment we were using as a classroom. It was from a school that had closed down in the city and was on its way to the incinerator when it was rerouted to our door. My delight in these chairs and desks was soon quelled when I saw the small pupils attempt to use them; it was as if they were park structures designed to teach climbing! Once the children had made their way into the over-sized chairs, their feet could no longer touch the ground, nor were they able to properly reach the surface of the desk. Utterly unacceptable and so degrading for the children that I removed them at once, with the children helping to tug and haul them right out the door and into the courtyard. From there, some of the laborers on the larger project helped to dispose of them entirely.

Here I sit at my cabin desk in a chair, which is just the right height, feeling a sense of great satisfaction to have that part behind me and to have fitted the children with furniture sized to them as well. Their faces held incredulity and elation on the day I placed the first small chair and table in the shaft of light falling through the window.

Tears sprang to my eyes just now as I remembered their joy, and then my mind jumped seamlessly to your joy on that day together. I went over that last afternoon in my head many times, and your joy was something I hoped to offer the children of San Lorenzo. Your genuine regard for others and your connection to the natural world. This was all held within the smooth stone you handed me that day. I placed that stone in the classroom on the opening day, and it lived perched on the high windowsill as a reminder to me each time I sought a refreshing view.

Looking out the window was something I did when I did not know what to do, and I found myself looking out the window quite often in those early days. There were so many moments when things arose that I did not yet have the answers to, and so placing your stone on the windowsill offered me both the sky and your hand as I pondered how to respond to the dear children at my skirts.

Now it appears I have gone off and left you yet again. You have only nearly arrived in the household, and I have boarded a ship to cross the ocean. Just these past few months for us to have begun our reconnection, and it must appear to you that I have once again intentionally chosen the children for whom this method was developed rather than you. When you read this, you will understand the stone I placed in your hand at the dock as it holds the promises we make to one another. It holds a future we will share.

I could not tell when you looked at me if you recognized the rock as having come from your own collection years earlier, the white stripes so prominent, but perhaps for a collector such as yourself, no longer rare. Yet to me, it is rare. It is potent and holds fractures without being at all broken.

If I were to have whispered something to you at your bedside as you fell asleep that last night or had placed a message inside the stone you now hold, I would have said, "I am right here. I have not gone anywhere."

Chapter Nine • 1912

There is a sense of weight upon us all as the ship navigates a smaller storm in the Gulf Stream. Certainly nothing of the magnitude of the previous one that pitched us all to dreadful sea sickness, as I have shared earlier in this epistle. And yet it influences me to feel this shift in the atmosphere, and I'll confess that this storm has hit my mood harder than my body.

I was previously quite chipper and even entertained a few dinners with the curious Americans. Mr. McClure's assistant translated so that I would be able to know their thoughts and stories and laugh at the right places. It is not an uncommon experience for me to feel on the outside of a group, all the while looking as though I am at the center. I am not certain how this comes to be. However, with this change in weather, I am aggrieved by the pattern and the thought that perhaps I have inadvertently passed this to you by the unusual way you have been raised, to be part of a family and yet separate from it. Not that Lorenzo and Angelina do not love you as their own—that would be false, as they adore you, and I could not support the idea for a single cresting wave. No, it is not about the loving environment in which you were raised, for I could have asked for no better.

Rather, it is about the way I imagine you may have felt different from Luca and Stella. Brought up as siblings, and yet the bond between the two of them that you must have sensed did not extend to you. Is this at all true, *mio caro*? I thought I read it on your face and in the way you spoke when you first arrived to live with us, and yet perhaps I am mistaken, and it is merely turmoil arising from the depths of the saltwater mixing into the story here where it should not. I wish now that I had asked you more frankly about how you came to understand that you were not, in fact, the Accardis' child but were instead mine. That I might have had the courage to face into the wind of the past as we began this new part of our relationship.

Perhaps then we leave it as an open question: Have you ever felt outside of a situation from the very middle of it? And if you have, is that simply a truth we carry as sentient beings? An experience we all share as we grow further distant from our ancestry, from our roots and rituals? Did the ancients ever feel it? Have we always wandered on our own journey, and it is only through civilization that we become momentarily disconnected from our own wholeness?

Perhaps all things look upside down when you first split them open.

The candle flickers, threatening to blow out and darken my cabin so that I will be interrupted from this train of thought. That, and the rising unease in my stomach as the waves grow larger and toss this mighty vessel as though it were a paper boat traveling along in a gutter. I will return to you in the morning with a fresh frame of mind and resume this tale properly.

Here on a fresh page, I begin again, drawing myself from the epicenter of the storm cloud outward to a place of more light. Instead of recounting the rather frightening events of this past storm, the ones where water came pouring into my cabin as other things poured out of my body, I shall jump forward half your life, for that is how long it was before I saw you again.

The call came unexpectedly from Lorenzo. He had taken his cart into the village to use the telephone there, and his voice was full of concern. It was again near your birthday, now the fourteenth, in the spring lambing season. The local doctor had died several weeks earlier and had not yet been replaced. When Luca fell from the barn roof and broke his arm, Lorenzo set it as best he could, but worried it was not healing properly. He was growing more concerned by the look of the arm, and I was the only doctor he could think of to call who might come to help.

I had held my agreement with myself to stay away and let you grow up without my vague presence in your life. With regular correspondence from Angelina, I was able to feel connected to your growth without potentially impairing it. And I allowed my work to consume all my waking hours, distracting me from the absence though not filling it.

Now that Lorenzo had made a direct invitation for me to come, I found myself invigorated by the prospect of seeing you again after all this time.

When I arrived at the farm, the sun was slanting across the fields, colors caught in the clouds above. I had the driver drop me at the end of the lane so that I would not arrive in any way grandiose, and I walked towards the farm with an expansive feeling of gladness that surprised me, given the circumstances.

I realize I have idealized the place in which you were raised, and I hope in the weeks and months to come, you will share your experience so that I may truly know how it was for you. But on that day, it was glorious. The light was falling along the fields scattered with patches of new green and old brown, with life beginning to spring up from the earth. The air was clear and fresh in my nose, and the radiance in the sky emanated; the clouds held more colors than a canvas.

I saw the family gathered in the pasture closest to the barn, your hunched figures standing around what I suspected was the patient. I could not make sense of why you would all be in the pasture, but I hitched my valise over my shoulder and began towards the group.

You looked up first, watching as I approached, and I regarded you fully for the first time in seven years. At fourteen, your height was to be expected, but the maturity of your face, the lankiness of your form, and the profound transformation you had made in the intervening years left me speechless. That agreement I had made with myself to stay away all this time seemed suddenly misguided, egregious even, and I tilted my head, considering the consequence of it.

"*Dottoressa!*" Lorenzo called as he saw me, and the rest of the family turned and watched me coming, unable to leave to greet me, rooted to their spots as though their positions were essential. There in the center was not Luca but, in fact, a sheep.

Then, all at once, Luca began talking about how Rosie had a lamb last night and had been laboring ever since, but the next lamb would not come, and now she could not even hold her head up anymore. I looked from Luca to Lorenzo for an understanding of the situation.

"Thank you for coming, *Dottoressa*," he said, now using his formal tone. "We awoke quite concerned about Luca's arm; however, when I returned from my call to you in the village, we had another misfortune. Rosie is Luca's sheep he has raised from a lamb." From these few sentences, I pieced together the shifting need and Luca's welfare as tied to both his arm and the well-being of his sheep.

I shifted my gaze to Luca and used my steady tone of suggestion when I requested that we look first at his arm and then attend to Rosie. With some agitation, he agreed.

Following an embrace from Angelina, I said, "Let us go inside the cottage where we can have a proper look." I turned to go, anticipating the others would follow, but Luca was not moving. When I turned back, I readily understood that the examination would be happening right there.

And so it was that his arm was unbound, revealing much discoloration. Upon further inspection, it was clear that the alignment of the bones had been done properly, but the binding and wooden splint had been ill-conceived.

"A fine job," I said, nodding at Lorenzo. "It will heal properly once I mix the plaster of Paris and cover the arm in such a way as to immobilize it. I have brought some in my valise, and we can mix it up in the kitchen." Again, I turned to go, and there was no motion in my wake.

"Ah, I see. Next, we must help Rosie, and then we will set the arm?" I asked Luca directly, who nodded in agreement.

I loosely bound his arm, though it offered little protection, and moved towards the laboring mother, who was indeed lying very still. Lorenzo offered the details, reporting with an undertone of resignation. Having seen many birthing seasons, he was aware of the risks and unfavorable outcomes.

Luca heard his father's tone as well, and his face fell. I understood then that you were all here for Luca rather than Rosie, and I rallied to join the cause, drawing out my stethoscope.

Rosie's heartbeat was there, but dim. Having never used a stethoscope on a laboring sheep before, I was unsure whether this was normal due to the layer of fleece or not at all normal and thus perhaps a bad sign, so I simply nodded, confirming she was alive and handed the apparatus to Angelina who was at my side.

In short order, two things were evident to me: that we needed to assist in the next birth and that the second lamb would not be born alive. What was not clear to me was that Lorenzo's assessment was accurate and that Rosie could not be saved.

I turned to face the family and began giving instructions on items to collect and preparations to make, sending them all off with the exception of Lorenzo and Luca whose arm hung at an odd tilt.

"We must deliver this lamb, and it will be hard to see." I paused there to check Luca's reaction.

Seeing he was unfazed, I continued. "I suspect something may have happened during the formation that is obstructing." He nodded, and I could see the spring lambing seasons of the past coming across his face. "We will need to help it pass," I said and stopped there.

"Thank you, *Dottoressa*," Lorenzo said simply.

Angelina came with the strong lye soap while you carried a bucket of warm water. I began scrubbing my hands and arms up to the high point to which I had rolled my sleeves. Angelina held out the towel, and I patted my hands dry, holding them up in the air as though I were going into surgery.

I looked at Lorenzo, and he dipped his head in agreement. We began.

Luca was at the head of the sheep, having shimmied his legs beneath her head while keeping his arm aloft. Lorenzo held up Rosie's tail as I sank my hand, wrist, and arm into the patient, who bleated weakly in response but didn't lift her head. Her first lamb came over to her then, moving nervously about until Angelina asked Stella, who had returned with the other supplies, to take him away, which she did. The little lamb continued to call to its mother in long, wrenching bleats as Stella carried him off.

My hand could feel the form of the next lamb inside Rosie, and I closed my eyes, using my fingers as instruments of sight. Legs to back-side, up the curve of it to where the neck should be, but instead, the head juts, and I falter.

Time grabbed me then, propelled me back to the point of your birth, how you arrived in the caul—a rare presentation and one thought to be auspicious. The midwife broke the caul, and your lungs inhaled their first breath, which filled them and started what would be a lifetime of labor.

I felt Angelina's hand on my shoulder and, at that moment, realized I had put my head down on the sheep's side, my arm still inside of her. The air was completely still, as though time had indeed temporarily stopped.

Do you remember what happened next? It was you who gently put your hand on my shoulder and, using your *nonna*'s find-your-feet gesture, silently urged me to take a hold of some part, to do something. This brought me to the task at hand. The next patch of time passed as I instructed Lorenzo where to add pressure from the outside. The sheep responded by kicking, and you stepped in to protect me from the hooves as I broke the bones in the small, dead lamb in order to deliver it. I believe you understood what I was doing, and from that perspective, I saw how barbaric it really was, though necessary in order to save the only life left. I also understood that Lorenzo knew this—steady, eyes trained on his own hands as though guiding them. After much effort from everyone and some tears from Luca, the lamb came out onto the grass.

"Is it alive?" Luca asked, his voice husky with dim, ill-placed hope. He shifted his legs, still holding the mother's head, as though he was preparing to rise, to come and hold the newborn.

You shook your head "no," and the movement of that gesture brought me to look at you—the deep feeling in the slack of your face, the sorrow in your eyes. This prompted me to wonder if the mother had lived through the event.

I moved to assess Rosie, and even before I settled beside her, I knew she was gone. My eyes went to Luca, who had his attention trained on the dead lamb, and then to Lorenzo and Angelina. They must be the ones to tell him, I thought.

I stepped back. With that opening, they both moved in, one on each side of Luca, Angelina taking care not to bump his arm as they wrapped him between them.

None of us spoke or moved, and silence fell. It fell the way night falls, the gradual coming over. The kind of silence that makes space for every other sensation—the light air crossing my skin, the smell of blood on the coat of the dead lamb, the impression of sticky fluid on the skin of my arm, the sound of Luca's quiet grief and the profound stillness, almost reverence for the life that might have been.

The moment stretched until the first lamb broke free from Stella and returned to the mother, pushing at her teats to nurse.

I lifted the broken body of the dead lamb out of the way of its sibling and held it to me, still warm. I felt my own body respond—my heart listening for its lost heartbeat. We are all interconnected, *mio caro*, don't let anyone tell you differently.

The first lamb nursing on the body of its lost mother added to the brokenness. I heard Stella's soft crying and felt you move to her; her sounds muted as she turned her face into your chest. We let the sorrow speak to us then as the light was leaving.

I held the lamb's body close as though I had known it a long while, as though I had grown it myself. Pulling the scarf from around my neck, I wrapped its body, holding it to me.

The first lamb had come to the end of the milk supply and went to nuzzle its mother, calling out in long bleats. It must have smelled death or sensed something wrong, for it then set off from its mother into the empty field, calling and calling, its cry echoing into the setting sun.

Just when I thought we could tolerate it no longer, the first notes of a melody came from Angelina, singing a goodbye hymn. The sky was awash with the colors of a sun passing the horizon, the golden glow catching the edges of the clouds and brightening the apricot, saffron, scarlet swatches that lay above the calling lamb. The contiguity of the beauty of the sky and the music with the harshness of the loss led me to close my eyes.

In that space between day and night, still holding the dead lamb, and with the mournful sound of Angelina's voice filling the cooling air, I allowed myself to understand what I had given up by leaving you—what I had taken from you—what we had lost, and I wept.

When Angelina finished, and I opened my eyes, I saw the first star in the night, the pinhole in the black cape of the sky—a sky that held the sheep's story now with my own—the losses accumulated.

What do you remember of that late afternoon? Were you aware of the way one loss brings up every other loss? Did you know I was grieving your lost childhood, or did you merely think me tender-hearted in the face of the natural cycle of life?

My heart is full of many questions, as you can see, and I must not permit myself to fill up the remaining leaves of paper with them. Instead, I shall hold them until the day when I present you with this. I will hold them knowing we will have all the time in the world to sit together, perhaps wrapped under your grandmother's crocheted blanket, tracing the slender threads with our fingers while we unwind this part of our story. This is, after all, only part of our story.

Dear boy, may this story—poorly told in patches, in fits and starts of resistance (for if I could tell you a better one, I would do it without tiring)—find its way into order, into a tale with enough meaning to shore you up and point you in the direction of your life's work.

Chapter Ten • 1912

News has come from the captain of the Cleveland through radiotelegraph as it passed us that the weather from New York has been lovely, which cheers us all immensely as we hope to be sailing into smoother seas. Our captain shared this with us at dinner last evening, and indeed today dawned beautifully with the full bright sun complementing the calm, magnificent sea. As we passed, I was able to see the Azores looking like fractured craters with small, simple white houses dotting the land. Standing at the deck rail, I felt myself travel there, waking in the modest bed and pulling on my dressing clothes to begin the day. Perhaps there is a cow to milk, and I grumble as the insistent cat awaiting breakfast turns the pail. I shoo her off and continue sending streams of warm milk to make a tune on the side of the metal bucket, my forehead resting on the flank of the beast.

Perhaps it is having just written you the tale of the lost lamb that sends my mind so readily to the farmyard, but I often think of the lives I am not now living. So many possibilities for one's life and to only live but one is something I must bear. And bear it well, for it is fully chosen.

When I returned home that night, I was flustered and unclear about how I would resume in the face of all that had surfaced. Seeing you as a young man had fuddled me, yet I once again held this happening close, and for reasons I still have not fully excavated, I did not share it with my mother.

In those interim years, we did not speak openly of you, though she baked a Pan di Spagna, well-soaked in a rum syrup and filled with both vanilla and chocolate custard, every March thirty-first. It would be on the table when I rose in the morning, and we would eat it for breakfast with cappuccino without ever saying your name.

The conversation we had when I returned from that afternoon was also oblique. She was in the sitting room in her usual chair, and I noted she held nothing in her lap—neither a book nor knitting—as I entered from hanging my coat and setting my valise in its proper place.

"You have been gone a long day," she stated, searching my face for information.

"Yes, it was a house call," I responded, noting how tired she appeared and wondering after the empty lap.

"Your father has gone off to bed," she said, answering the unasked question. She regarded me then with her old look of evaluation, and her voice softened when she asked, "What do you need, *tesora*?"

At that, my composure slid, and I longed for the days when I could be enveloped by her, as I had seen Luca be held by his parents. "*Mammina*," I said simply.

"Yes," she replied, patting her skirts that I should go and lay my head upon her lap as I once had.

Perhaps this is how you felt the first night your cries brought me to your bedroom door? Torn between wanting the comfort and believing yourself grown enough to do without it. Or perhaps the way I felt that night at your door is the way she felt seeing my pain then. Torn between wanting to comfort and believing in me to do it on my own.

Either way, I did not let her in, did not share that I had seen you again after so long. Instead, I made tea.

I made a pot of tea and covered it with my homemade tea cozy. It was the one with the star fabric that had been my curtains until I needed it for my mother's birthday present. I always used that tea cozy when I wanted to say something to my mother without words. Sometimes it was "And such is the untamed creature I have always been," which I would offer by way of apology for a transgression rather than an excuse. Or "Shall we simply have a laugh of it?" when I felt one of us was unnecessarily peeved over something or other. On that night, I believe I was saying, "I do need you still."

Though I did not share my confusion and heartache, having tea and sitting together in our comfortable chairs was enough.

The next day, quite unexpectedly, I was asked to travel to Messina, where there had been a terrible earthquake that left sixty small children without families. Queen Margherita, who had visited the original Casa several times, called upon me to help the nuns in the Franciscan convent to set up a little school following my method, named Casa on Via Giusti. It was a fine time for me to have something larger than myself to focus on, and so I agreed.

At first, the children were bereft and succumbed to crying, unable to eat or sleep. The nuns and I had our hands full—rocking, soothing, holding, and feeding these *bambinos*, who now had no one. The few moments in the night when my eyes closed, I sent prayers through my breath, for I admit, Mario, I thought I had gotten in beyond my abilities. I was a scientist, a clinician—what did I know of soothing those with shattered lives?

I had grown up in a life of privilege where my every wish was met. My fundamental human needs were attended to by my loving parents, and I wanted for nothing. I had no worries and no wishes. I had offered you the same in the home of the Accardis, and though it had pulled me apart, reliving your birth and realizing the true weight of the loss in our separation these past years, it had also confirmed my belief in the placement. To grow up on the land, living in the natural cycle of every day with caring adults, is a privilege these children had lost.

Those first nights in Messina, my mind turned the situation over and over in an attempt to solve what was before me. Instead of answers, I continued to find the pain and suffering of those around me, arrested by the pungent smell of the ward where the cots lay, and the bleak fabric dangling in front of the windows as though imitating a home. I became turned around by the calls and cries throughout the night, the clear and evident misery with no definitive action to take—no splint, tonic, or treatment. Going to the bedside of a crying child, I stood and regarded them with all the uselessness of a coat rack. I had neither the experience nor the skills to manage what was before me, and though I imitated my mother's actions, remembering what she did when I was ill, none of the head stroking made one whit of difference.

Then one night I picked up Sophia, who, based on her piercing cries, was reliving the moment of the earthquake each night. She had watched as the walls of her home crushed her parents and two siblings. She herself was buried by rubble yet saved by being thinner than the beam that fell parallel rather than across her small body. I took her into my arms that night, and as she burrowed into me to find asylum, the way an animal might, I spontaneously began humming a song your *nonna* would sing to me when I was ill or overwrought. As I hummed, I began to rock, and her cries abated. After a few times through, she had quieted fully, and I moved to place her back on the cot. This movement roused her, and she began to cry out once again, stirring those near her. I quickly returned to my original position, humming and rocking once again. This pattern continued until I conceded and kept her in my arms.

I thought my arms would break for the long time in this fashion, and through that discomfort, that rising pain in my muscles, came a small despair. Perhaps I had imagined I could do something that, in the end, I could not do. What if I could not do it? What if Sophia never soothed, never stopped the shrill calls in the night that woke all the others and left the ward weeping—including the nuns and me? Had I been moved by pride when asked by the Queen herself to attend to such a mission?

It was not a school that was needed here, but a nursery or a White Cross to heal the spirits broken within the little ones. What did I know of healing in this way? What did I know of broken?

When I asked that question with those words that night, filled with doubt as I was, it came to me with certainty. You see, Mario, leaving you, I knew everything I needed to know about being broken, and from there, I understood what needed to happen next. What had moved me out of my own grief and loss was service and, specifically, service to others.

The next day, after the morning meal, I gathered the older children around me. They sat settled in their fresh outfits with hands and faces cleaned, their hunger satisfied, ready to give me their attention. I told them that I needed their help. With this, they tilted their heads in interest. I waited until Georgio asked: "Please, *Dottoressa*, what can we help you with today?"

"It is no small matter, Georgio," I told him. "Are you sure you would like to hear?"

He nodded eagerly, and the others nodded as well.

"Today is the day we must begin the mending." I sat with my hands in my lap and my back straight, as though that was surely enough of an explanation.

The children looked from me to each other, and when they found no further information there, they prompted Georgio, who had become a bit of a spokesperson for the group. "Mending?" he said simply.

"Yes," I said just as simply in reply.

Georgio didn't wait for his cue from the group but launched in to ask, "What is mending?"

"Mending is when you fix something that is torn or broken," I answered.

"What is torn or broken?" he asked.

So many things were torn and broken, *mio caro*, but I was not about to overwhelm dear Georgio, and so I waited to reply. In that silence, the children began looking around.

"Sophia's blanket is torn," Marta pointed to the little bed with the tumble of blanket, the edge of which was frayed, and she was correct—it was torn!

From there, all the children began to call out what they saw that needed mending. Luckily, I had a stash of paper and a pencil in my apron, and I began writing down their observations. When they slowed and stopped, I offered to read back the list. They were all sitting up as straight as I was now, looking on in earnest as I read their contributions slowly and carefully to note the importance of each one.

"There is indeed a lot of mending needed," I said to finish. Then we sat and let the sounds of all those items fall around us and loop in our ears.

After a moment of quiet, one child said softly, "I could fix the table."

"May I write your name next to it—that you will fix the table?" and the child nodded with conviction.

"I know how to sew. I could fix Sophia's blanket," said Marta, and when I didn't move, she added, "You may write my name next to it."

And thus was my first experience with older children, for all of these young orphans I had gathered to me were between six and nine years old. From that one meeting, they began to work on repairs of all manner within the convent and, through the days and weeks that followed, began themselves to mend.

At our next meeting, I tasked each of the older children with the care of a younger one; and full of accomplishment from the items they had put to right, they took their young charge in hand, leading them places and prompting them to begin participating in the care of the convent through small deeds like picking flowers and closing the door carefully so the repaired latch would remain in place.

The persistence of required attention helps us all keep our minds off our losses. And I will not veil that sentence but say plainly that it was only consuming work such as this that kept me from feeling the distance between us and anguishing over it.

The children missing their parents met me missing my child in a collision of need that resulted in days of reconstruction until we were all sleeping through the night again. Days spent mending in Messina, finding ground together and then digging in it, the children speaking charms to keep away the rot.

This experience changed me. I understood unequivocally that I was a teacher—and that improving the life of a children across all age groups was my life's work

Now the light on the water outside my portal is luminous, and it has been a week since I left you. Writing this down in a series of pages to you is seeing me through this next separation, and I remind myself regularly that this is not like the last time, the last time when its duration and end were unknown to us. This time we have an understanding that I will return in short order so we can mark the passing days on the calendar and find each new one with fortitude. I have begun this practice myself—not as a way to rush time forward, but instead as a way to mark it in the passing, to be alive to right now, and also know that as each day passes, we are one day closer to being back together again.

You have not yet spoken to me of that time when I was away—those years between your seventh birthday and your fourteenth when I left you to grow in the unfettered care of Angelina and Lorenzo, and so I do not yet know your experience. I will tell you, though, receiving your letter those months later when I returned from Messina brought me great joy.

In the most forthright manner, you established your comfort with the truth of our relationship. Following my visit to help with Luca's arm, you had approached Lorenzo and asked him to tell you the level truth, and he did so—at fourteen, he rightly decided it was yours to know, as he did so without discussing it with me.

The spring and summer then passed with the work of the farm as a priority, and I wonder how often you turned over the idea of writing to me. Was it much on your mind, or as you stated in the letter, prompted by your desire to continue your education, or both? Upon reading that,

I felt immense gratitude to Angelina for prioritizing your education in the midst of her busy household. This, she had assured me, would not fall by the wayside, and thus the books I sent over the years were put to good use.

Among other things, however, I believe you were writing to me for confirmation of our relationship, though I have no evidence of that fact. I felt the impetus to respond directly to your letter and wish I'd had the capacity to do so the very day I received it.

I remember that day, feeling my mother's eyes upon me, adhered there by the element of curiosity, and I must have flushed under her gaze. Having no context for what had come to me in the day's post, I could feel her mind travel far and wide, embellishing invented stories as she watched me. I wish I had asked her what she was imagining. Instead, I folded the letter carefully and pressed it into my apron pocket, returning to the task of shelling the peas leftover from summer, carefully placing the empty pods into a separate bowl from the plump round result of some farmer's garden-tending. Your *nonna* was most resolute when she set her mind, and I knew she had determined not to inquire, and so I let the tension fill the pea bowl, ignoring the silent urgings to confide in her. Piles of sweet, green peas gathered in the time that passed with the smell of apples filling the air, fresh from the morning market and being peeled by my mother beside me, her hand slow with the knife now, the peels in bits rather than her customary unbroken spirals. Here is another moment I wish to retrieve from time and make a different choice, one that turned toward her in that opening rather than away.

Instead, I hoarded this intimacy with you for myself. Later, when I was in the quiet of my own chamber, I took your letter out again and read the words that had been written by your very own hand. I brushed the paper with my fingers as though able to feel you there. You had become a literate young man capable of beautiful lettering, articulate and clear, much like Angelina's. You asked after my health and spoke of Luca's arm now strong and the lamb now months grown. You did not offer all the details, but from what you did write, I could picture you nursing the lamb in those early days—filling a bottle with warm milk and chasing him across the spring field. I imagined you mounding hay around him for the drop in temperature in the evenings and lying with him awhile so he did not become despondent from lack of kinship. Then frolicking in the lengthening days that followed to offer him a much-needed connection as he grew through spring into summer.

The letter acted as a crystal ball, and all this I saw merely by stroking the rough writing paper. I reviewed the text again, more slowly this time, and smiled to read you had named the lamb Angelo—messenger of God. There was much inside of what you had written there for me to review, but the image of you tending to one untended by his mother was arresting. Your kindness and care for Angelo in the wake of his mother's death spoke volumes, and so perhaps it was indeed God's divine plan that I had come that afternoon, that I was part of that story.

When, at the close of the letter, you wrote that your time there was coming to an end, my heart skipped as it had the first time I read it. And then your final sentence, written separately from all the rest: "I would stay with you, if you would have me."

Just the previous winter, I had completed the first training course organized by Mr. and Mrs. Alexander Graham Bell, Anne George, and of course Mr. Sam McClure, with sixty-five students traveling all the way from America to attend. Even as the course drew to an end, I knew I was not done with America, and so it was not much of a surprise when later they asked me to visit. This invitation came after the incident with Rosie, and so my mind was traveling to other places when your message arrived. It is remarkable to me, though, how much the world stopped when I read those words on the page: "I would stay with you, if you would have me."

It was autumn by then; the hay crackling to be cut, and I troubled over the response. My mother's health was in decline, and I was not clear what was the right next step. I took many walks, especially at night so my brow of consternation could furrow unchecked. I would walk to Villa Borghese and seek out the peace that dwelled there, separate from the city's pace and free of mental traffic. My limbs would go slack, and I could feel the weight fall off me as I walked, the log jam of mind releasing as I moved.

I was much troubled by my mother's health. One detected the dwindling by knowing her on the inside rather than any flagrant outward signs, though the slowness of her movements would surely have tipped off anyone who knew her at all. What was notable to me was how little she went out of doors in the last year of her life, and so even her closest of friends did not see her diminish in the way they might have were she to have been in motion. Instead, sipping tea, or gathering the knitted items for the less fortunate into piles based on size, did little to reveal her reduced energy in the way I felt it. Her hands grew unsteady, and she attempted to conceal this by retiring her sewing needle, concentrating instead on thick hats made with wide needles that would be well-suited for those in the far north. Thus, she was able to disguise the rapidity with which the end approached. I see this now and receive it with equal parts gratitude and regret.

"Come walk with me, *cara Madre*," I would say to her then, but she would shake her head and whisk her hand back and forth, sending me out the door without an excuse or explanation—just that simple 'go on' gesture.

One night I took my unrest and growing sense of foreboding for an evening stroll. The change I sensed in my mother had me increasingly disconcerted, and I had not yet replied to your letter, though I carried it in my pocket. I needed to walk it all off, move through it, get inside it to understand it all. What began as an amble grew to a brisk pace as I went to the back side of Villa Borghese, where the trees were thick. The deciduous among them were undressing, and with the prompt of a rustle from above, my eyes flitted up to the high branches. And there it was, still and poised, looking down at me so that our eyes locked. How is it possible the cosmos lives inside an owl's ink-drop eyes—intent, unblinking, portentous? I stood transfixed as we remained with our eyes locked, and through his gaze, I was transported.

I keep writing about these mysttttical experiences, *mio caro*. I hope it is long into knowing me that you read this, for otherwise, I fear you may be most unsettled by what you are encountering on these typed pages, the repeating *t* being the least of it!

I do wonder, though, have you had such a moment yet with another living creature? One that takes your breath and folds it like origami into the shape of something you did not know until that moment? If you have not, it is my hope for you that one day you do know such a power from outside yourself—a power linked to the wider universe and the way we are all woven together, able to know and feel beyond the limits of our own skin.

I will confide in you now that at that moment in the park, I knew my life was about to change in significant ways. What I did not know was the context of the change; it was a queer combination of expansive joy and contracting sorrow. This feeling was so strong that I became rattled. I clutched my chest in a reflexive response, and this unsettled the owl so that we broke our gaze. When we did so, the sensation in my feet returned so that I could feel the ground beneath me, and I walked quickly on. I walked and walked that night, reconciling the coming of my mother's death, now known to me less as a cognitive thought and more as a sensation.

I fear I have not dwelt enough in this manuscript on the ways my mother ruddered me through the entire course of my life. And yet it is true that there would not be enough pages to capture her importance. Perhaps instead, I shall tell you of our last day together, which in many ways holds the sum of us.

It was December, and the cold had crept into the city so that my mother shivered more than was comfortable for either of us. On that last day, I had nearly every blanket we owned piled on her, and that was a considerable number, given her prolific way with knitting needles. I sat in the chair bedside, reading to her from the book of poems I mentioned earlier, as they often gave us much to think about and settled us both. Your *nonna* made humming sounds at particular parts, and I knew from years of reading to one another when she was highlighting a single, delicious word and when it was the image being created by the slew of words.

When I stopped to prepare lunch, she shook her head no at the choices I offered. Her gaze set out the window. I brought a tray of small plates anyway, as it was our favorite—to pretend we were on a picnic by having many selections rather than one large course. When I placed the tray on the table, it rattled, and Mother startled as though she had been sleeping.

"Did I wake you?" I asked, peering over the blankets into her withered face. Her lips spread into a smile I recognized, the one that noted the heaviness of my footsteps or imprudent attack with a paring knife. "Yes, that was loud," I admitted, and her face further softened until there came a small laugh. To see my mother's face tucking out from the mounds of blankets, in delight, had me laughing as well. It was the type of laughter that begins small, like a quiet first note, *diminuendo* that then slowly builds *forte*, until I am laughing loud enough to shake my belly, tears coming down my mother's cheeks. This laughter brought back a flurry of all my indelicate moments in rapid succession that had registered on my mother's face, from eggs spilling out of the basket I was swinging too rigorously, to the Chiaravalle kitchen door slamming, to last month when I hurried into the sitting room and my shoe caught on the edge of the rug propelling me into my mother's reading chair where she sat dozing. She startled awake, and seeing me as the object that had crashed into her brought that very same smile. We laughed that day as well.

Perhaps it was that last scene, and the thought that we would not have that moment again, that turned my laughter slowly into tears, moving from its natural *crescendo* to *pianissimo*, from *allegro* to *grave*.

I leaned down, resting my head next to my mother's where our tears met and were absorbed by her pillow. I closed my eyes and saw so many of these times across the arc of my life, the times her mere presence was of comfort to me, and I absorbed this one into the collection.

Soon though, I felt her trembling and lifted my head to regard her. She was shivering. Despite the heaps upon her, her body could not warm.

Thus, I brought her a pot of tea tucked in the star cozy I had made for her some thirty-odd years earlier. On that day, I think perhaps I was saying, "I love you so much I would cut curtains for you."

I sat on the edge of the bed with the tea tray set on the side table and plucked the cozy off the pot with aplomb, looking to her for a reaction. My heart fell then when I saw that her eyes had gone to another place. The cozy fell from my hand, and I moved to her, climbing under all those covers to the frail body she inhabited. "You are still here, *mia cara*," I whispered into her ear, my arms thrust around her, holding her to me. "You are still here," I repeated, tears piercing. When she did not respond, I pulled her closer to me, and with my lips on her cheek, I called her back, "*Mammina.*"

Before she even turned to me, I knew this would work. I knew this would stir the part of her that had always responded when I called her this way, which I reserved for times when I really needed her.

And she came.

"Mimi," she exhaled more than said it.

"Tell me what to do," I answered.

Slowly, and with the last of her breath, she said, "And so the child becomes the mother now. It is time."

When my father came in later, we were still in this position. Mother had gone, and I had my head buried into her shoulder.

This is how it was decided that you would come to live in Rome. I pressed into her body as she left hers, as she sailed off from me, and my mind shifted to Chiaravalle, our farm with light cresting the horizon enough to see the dew. The feeling was a solid, most trusting feeling, as though there was no cause for concern, nothing unusual, just another day dawning with the teakettle whistling on the stove. It was a sense of the rhythm when one is in the balance of life, the clock gently ticking, the usual bird at the windowsill, and then you came into the kitchen with the eggs, and we began cooking them. Mind you, this was not something we had yet done at the time, but I can hardly instill in you how commonplace it felt in my mind.

So, when my father arrived at the bedside and roused me, I rose from my mother's bed and announced, "Papa, it is time for the child to come home." I almost said "my child," but at the last moment, I wavered off of it, landing on a definite article rather than a possessive pronoun. From this, you should only gather that I was shaken and not prepared should he have an unfavorable response.

As it was, my timing was most awful. Of course, from his perspective, he came in from a workday to find his wife had passed and his only child curled alongside her corpse. Naturally, he was much disquieted at what he had found and slid to his knees at the bedside, where he remained until darkness fell. He held the hand of my mother until she was taken from the house. The customary weeks of grieving and preparations followed, within which we began as strangers and ended as the closest of comrades.

I say this because there was some phenomenon that occurred between us in the absence of my mother that could not exist in her presence. This did not remove the sharp ache I felt each day upon waking and re-remembering that she was gone, a repeated experience that took a shorter and shorter time to occur as the weeks went on. Those first mornings I drifted innocently from sleep to find myself unconsciously listening for her downstairs, my nose lifting to smell something delicious coming from the kitchen. You might imagine the pain of having to remember it, again and again, each day—that she was gone forever, that the only smells to rise from the kitchen now would be my doing. I admit that I spiraled into a young place that first week, nestled beneath the covers and crying in deep grief—a child who has lost her mother.

It straightens me to write that sentence, realizing this has been your life up until now, and I resolve, over the remaining years we have together, to remedy any loss you may have experienced. There is no one near the caliber of my mother, and I should never imagine being such a person, but I can aspire to fill you with the love I feel for you. For you have brought me back from the despair I felt in those early days following her death. The idea that I would agree to your proposal was a spark that lifted me from my bedclothes and propelled me to the kitchen to begin a new chapter.

To change one thing is to change everything. A truth that repeats the way the sun appears each day—never in the same way, yet consistently and without question. This I say to you so that you may find acceptance even in your bleakest hour, as I did in mine.

Your *nonna* is buried in a sarcophagus in a monument on Campo Verano. Perhaps upon my return, we shall visit this cemetery, wandering together into the center of Rome and through the inviting paths of Campo Verano. And following that, as the light is leaking from the sky, then on to Villa Borghese in search of the owl, though he may wait to meet you until he has a message for you. Instead, perhaps we will visit your *nonna*'s favorite tea shop near the Biblioteca Nazionale Centrale di Roma and go on to see *Sig.* Rapport for all the latest additions there at the library. Many adventures ahead, *mio caro*, many adventures ahead.

It is nearly time for me to retire for the night, and so I shall finish this leaf of paper. The journey is nearly at its end, and that means we must complete this one-sided conversation. Perhaps I will tidy the pages and read through them tonight to see if there are any important pieces missing that I must add prior to the close of this edition and the end of this sea voyage. I am quite certain that my return trip will not be nearly so productive as this one has, for after so many days of travel and translation and teaching, I shall surely be no better than a mop-head set out onto the deck to watch the clouds pass.

For now, I bid you goodnight in hopes you are well tucked in and that you and your *nonno* are getting on well. Though age has reduced it, he still has a laugh that can startle, and I hope you have come to find it contagious rather than offensive. He means well, *mio caro*. He is not mocking you when the hoots burst out of him, merely expressing delight that took me until this year to understand. I tell it to you now so you will be out ahead of it, though I realize upon typing it that it is a rather foolish notion for you are perceptive beyond your years and surely have already settled on his good intent.

Instead, I will close tonight with this small scene from the days leading up to your coming when I was creating a room for you in your grandmother's sewing room, the very place you are sleeping as I write this. We are not a family of grand means, nor are we humble, and I hope you do not feel less esteemed to learn your room was a sewing room, for it is the very best room in the house. That, I think, is why my father relegated it as my mother's room from the outset of our time there. I remember how, having already been inside on several occasions, he led us through narrating the spaces and their functions. "And this, my dear," he said with a flourish, bowing a bit as he gestured to the open doorway, "will be for you to use as you wish." His delight in having been able to afford a home spacious enough for such a thing was entirely transparent, and my mother, who rarely indulged him about most things, actually flushed a little, blinking her eyes slowly at him as though communicating through a secret language.

How I can go on, Mario! I was set to write only one small moment, and now the wick is low, and I have not yet shared about how your room came to be. Let us close this by imagining your room as it is now, with the thick spread sewed by your *nonna's* hands over the years with all the patches of my favorite cloth. Someday I will walk you through each one, and if the time has not come before I am very old, then you may use it as a test of my mind to be sure it is of continued good health! In there is a piece of the blanket you were wrapped in at the convent when you were born. Before you arrived, I purchased fabric to match it in order to sew you a proper pillowcase. Your *nonno* noticed right away when he came to inspect the room for your arrival. Then he stood long at the doorway, his eyes growing moist. I thought perhaps he was picturing my mother there and that the subject of his grief was her passing, but I discovered that was not the source at all. After this quiet pause, he disappeared and then returned with a book, which he placed next to your bed. As I went to inspect it, he stopped me, taking my arm so that I looked at him.

"This book my father gave to me. Now I pass it on to the boy Montessori—it is for his eyes, not yours." That was all he said of it, and I respected that request, not even glancing to learn the title. Your room was ready. It was time for you to come home.

Chapter Eleven • 1913

The sun fashioned the day here on deck following another choppy night, and I am weary of the trip to the point where I perked up at the announcement that we are close to our destination and will soon be arriving at the New York City port in the United States of America. I have sailed across the sea! Now I am on one side and you on the other, sea and sky stretched out between us, connecting us on these days ahead of walking on separate ground.

The group that Mr. McClure has enticed to sign on as part of the American Montessori Society lobbied for a final celebration tonight, which will involve music and dancing. I must admit, *mio caro*, that I found this idea inviting, and I woke looking forward to the affair. There is something about festivities that lightens the heart and enlivens the spirit, even when the body has had a strain on it. I leaped from bed this morning in anticipation.

However, shame rose across my face at breakfast when I learned of the Austrian stowaway found close to death down in the hold between the trunks stored there. He has been brought to the infirmary, and they are hoping to restore him since he has not had more than the bread he brought from Naples. When he snuck on board there, he imagined this vessel would stop, as it usually does, in Genoa. Instead, he has endured the terrible storm at sea and rocky waters since, only just now having been found, with great doubt that they will revive him. This has the effect of quelling my excitement about the evening as it reminds me most viscerally that we are a world of fortunate and unfortunate. It has long been true that I come from the fortunate and, when interfacing with the unfortunate, feel the cut of that injustice deep within my being, as though I do not know how to tolerate the dissonance.

I once would fall headlong into the sorrow of that divide with bouts of railing against it, only to fall back, defeated. It is something greater than my person that our world is so divided into those born into means and those born without and the great condemnation of society of those living without. Even on this very ship, the whispers amongst the attendees of the extravagant breakfast repast disparaged the man on board who, in this moment, is fighting for his very life. This created a bile that soured the fruit, entering my mouth to where I needed to excuse myself. Although not before I managed to alienate myself from the present company by remarking on the position of privilege from which they condemned a dying man. I said this in Italian, so it is possible that some of the Americans enlisted by Mr. McClure were unable to receive the full meaning of my words. I am sure, however, that through my posture and tone, they were able to ascertain the general meaning of my message. I express no regret here. If they all decide to remove their names from the Montessori Society list now, I will not be disappointed, for what remains more important is that I must not disappoint myself.

You will learn this, Mario, that the moments of disappointing yourself stay with you long beyond those of disappointing others. In the end, it is you to whom you must answer, and I stand with the stowaway firmly on this matter. One does what they need to do to survive, and when it is of no harm to others, then what is all the lip flapping about? Self-aggrandizement, and that is all. I have had my time thinking myself better than others, but as I have told in previous pages, the fortuitous experience of getting pregnant with you brought an end to that chapter. Perhaps I shocked you there using the word pregnant rather than a more acceptable euphemism, and if so, please know that I use it intentionally, as I am not clear why there must be shame in this process, why it must be hidden.

I am aware that everyone has a hidden story, like Business, like the children of the earthquake, and that to judge without knowing is more foolish than chopping the potato plant at the stem without harvesting the goodness grown below. My greatest fear is that the society forming around my name would seek to cater to the already privileged, forgetting those of San Lorenzo, who were the very ones who taught us this method of education to begin with. Will it reach all the children of America? Will there be access for those who would be well-served by a dignified education, or will it be reserved for the affluent without further thought of the children without means?

Mio caro, please forgive this long rant that may perhaps be the result of living in the opulence of these past two weeks. I understand now that it has stifled my awareness of injustice evident all around me. I have enjoyed some of the indulgences—the expansive cabin with the bed large enough for two, the fruit bowl refreshed and always overflowing with sweetness, and this blessed typewriter which has offered itself as my vehicle for delivering you this tale. All the while, there lay below an unfortunate soul who had nothing and had sacrificed everything in his efforts to return home. Perhaps he has a child such as yourself, a boy of some years approaching adulthood who waits for him, wondering if his papa will return. This has put tears in my eyes, and I realize that I am overwrought with my decision to leave you so soon after our reunion.

"Come in, come in," I said just now when there was a knock on the cabin door. Brushing my eyes with my dress sleeve, I was suddenly aware of the melancholic disposition that had fallen over me. Into the cabin bustled a small man dragging my steam trunk, announcing that it was time to begin packing and that he would return later in the day to remove it. Adding, as he shuffled backward towards the still open door, not to forget to leave out my finest for the event this evening, as I would be honored.

I am unclear what alerted him, but he turned a perceptive gaze upon me. "Are you not pleased to be honored?"

"Oh, yes," I began working to recover an acceptable narrative. Yet there was something about the realness, the earnestness of his face that had me trailing off before fully reviving. We stood considering each other while my mind flashed to the Austrian man, the lavish breakfast, the circumstances that separate humanity.

"You have been working hard," he gestured at the typewriter and the pile of pages gathered there. "Perhaps it would be all right to celebrate just a little?"

By skillfully making the last part a question, he activated a discernment process that elevated my thinking on the matter. Once he saw this, he began moving backward to exit. As he did so, he stumbled a bit over the lip at the doorway, and his round hat tipped over his left ear, prompting him to take it off, enact a small dance in recovery, and wave his hat with aplomb for my amusement. With that, my mood instantly shifted, and a small laugh erupted from me. He was pleased and joined me, so that we were both chuckling together when a gust of wind came through the cabin, causing the door to slam between us.

This was followed by his gentle rap and, without pausing for my invitation, a cracking of the cabin door with just the sliver of his face appearing there to offer his sincere apology for the hasty and inelegant departure. I smiled widely in reassurance, telling him that, quite to the contrary, his visit had been the highlight of my day.

I suppose this is my cue to begin packing and to prepare for the anticipated events ahead in America, but I could not resist reporting this exchange to you lest you worry after your mother as despondent. The world is indeed troubling, and yet to deny the moments of pleasure serves no one. There is much work to do on behalf of the world's children, and if I am unable to share small joys amidst the sorrow, then

I will likely not live long enough to effect significant change for the next generation. The man discovered below deck was once a child who may have been taught to believe that he was less worthy than others, as all the girls in my school class who never finished were taught to believe that they were less worthy than the boys who walked with their shoulders back and their chests pumped out, certain they were superior. No one is superior, *mio caro*, and at the very same time, everyone is extraordinary. We all hold within us the ability to make something new, as the porter reminded me so clearly. And so, I shall do my part. I shall dutifully pack my trunk and ready myself to bring the idea to a new land. I shall steel myself in case there is no reception there and they should believe my idea foolish or reckless—to see in the child the promise for future generations rather than something to be stifled.

Regardless, in the end I shall, for the first time, be returning to you.

I am hoping when we reach the shore that there will be a telegram holding news of you and your *nonno*. Perhaps you will have written a few lines for me to enjoy, to hold me up as I face this new country, making speeches in a language few here speak, being asked questions without understanding their meaning and requiring the assistance of constant translation.

Catastrophe and education are two words I have learned in English on this voyage, and their juxtaposition urges me to pull out this sheet of paper from the typewriter and begin another book on the calamity we seem to be on the brink of in education. I tried in my best broken English to express this to the man who taught me the word "catastrophe," but I fear none of what I said translated. He kept an even smile in place while I spoke most passionately, but I am certain that if he had understood my meaning, his face would have darkened, or at the very least, his eyebrows would have come together in a union of displeasure; for you see, I was railing against the catastrophic state of education in the world and how what we need is an education for peace. Perhaps I will name the book this when I do write it; though prior to that endeavor, prepare myself to do a better job of articulating my convictions.

For now, however, what I shall make peace with is the end of this unsightly pile of papers that has accumulated over the course of the voyage. Mr. McClure, when he heard of the ill-fated demise of my paperweight at dinner one night, made a show of gifting me with a new one, pulling it from behind his back as though completing a magic trick. It was rather riveting to watch him accomplish this in the tight quarters of the table without disturbing the glassware or sending the edge of his plate flying. His replacement paperweight was a ship's anchor made of bronze, and it gleamed in the palm of his hand as he held it out proudly.

Knowing my part in the magic show, I clapped my hands with delight as though doves had been brought from mid-air. The others joined me, and Mr. McClure actually blushed as he transferred the treasure from his own hand safely into mine. It has a satisfying weight to it and a ruggedness that appeals, and so I have set it down upon this story to anchor it.

A wise poet once wrote a poem entitled "How We Use Sorrow to Get Rid of Sorrow." I wish I had the volume at hand on this journey so that I might reread it and remember with greater clarity what surreptitious message was hidden in between the words and lines as they fluttered down the page. Interesting that I can remember the shape of the poem better than the content, but perhaps that was the intent—that the intrigue of the title combined with the shape of the writing might be the most unforgettable parts.

I suppose this poem is coming to mind now because that is the next bit of the story, how I used the sorrow of losing my most precious mother to rid myself of the sorrow of being separated from my most precious child.

And you have rid me of sorrow, Mario.

This is not to say that I do not deeply miss my mother every day, only that I have not sunk into sorrow. There is a temptation when that sort of grief beckons to join it fully, to set up house with it and care for it as you once did the living. I have felt this myself and watched my father toy with the idea as well. Without applying pressure to you, I will say candidly that it is your appearance in our house that has kept us both from succumbing to this gravitational pull. What is true is that you are very much like your grandmother, and perhaps (and I am just realizing this as I write it) when we are in your presence, we feel in some way as though we are in her presence.

The way you walk slowly down the stairs, letting your hand float gently along the banister. The way you tap your hard-boiled egg vertically from one hemisphere to another, rather than along the equator, as Papa and I are wont to do. Is that the way Lorenzo and Angelina crack their eggs, or did you come to that all on your own? I shall have to ask them the next time we are all together to celebrate my return from America. They have invited us to the farm and promised to roast a pig for the occasion. I imagine you will enjoy wrestling with Luca again in the dust of the barnyard. Do you miss that? You have traded your old life for one which, by all standards, is fairly sedate, and yet you seem content with it.

I have done it again, fallen to asking you questions you are not here to answer and then surmising the answer. Perhaps the journey has gone on so that I am now in an abstract conversation with myself—both asking and answering. Between that and so many meals spent in the company of Americans speaking rapid English, I worry that I may lose the art of conversation before long. Perhaps by the time we are reunited, I will only be able to stand before you swaying, speaking of the catastrophe in education!

I shall turn from all that now to share my impressions of the day you moved to Rome and how clear it all is to me these months later. Putting it down here will capture it, though I am sure in this case that will not be necessary, for I shall remember it all my days.

Angelina had sent a post letting us know the day of your arrival and that you insisted on coming alone. It seemed you were not to be convinced to allow them to accompany you on the short journey from the country, and though the note was in her usual manner—short and to the point—I did sense both an ambivalence and a pride in your readiness to take this trip alone. I have not yet imagined your parting with the family there, though I could put some pieces together to do so from minor stories you have told since your arrival.

One such comes to mind—the evening I heard you telling your *nonno* of the last night's dinner at the farm. You were in the sitting room together as I was passing by, and you were planning my send-off for this very trip, creating it in your minds as a festive affair. When your *nonno* asked if you had yet seen a party snapper, you replied that they were at your sendoff dinner as well.

"Mimi enjoys the surprise of the snapper, but even more, she likes the fortune that you find on the inside. Did the ones at your party have fortunes?" *Nonno* asked you.

I admit that I paused then to listen, though, at the time, I did not mean to eavesdrop, only to admire the relaxed way you spoke to one another.

"Yes, they did, yet it was not a party for only the family that was there..." you replied, though the last words caught on your tongue as though furry rather than smooth. You began to correct it, but your *nonno* moved in seamlessly with another question.

"Did glitter fall on the table when they snapped?" he asked.

Relieved, you went on, "Why yes, glitter and a tissue paper bit that, when carefully unfolded, became a crown!"

"Oh yes, those are the very nicest!" And something about his tone let me know that he himself had sent those party snappers, for I cannot imagine where in the countryside Lorenzo and Angelina would have come by them, nor why they would have even considered spending a sum of money on something so relatively useless. "You are a well-loved young man then to have the very best snappers at your send-off!" he continued enthusiastically.

I wish I might have been bold enough to peer around the corner and see your face. I had a clear vision of your *nonno*'s face as he said that; however, I cannot yet hear you speak and picture how your face is arranged. In time though, *mio caro,* in time.

"Luca did not know it was a hat, and he tore his as he was rushing to find his message," you responded, deflecting the comment.

"Ah yes, that is easy to do. Mimi did that her first time and cried bitterly, saying she should have mine instead." Papa laughed as he remembered the occasion, and my mind immediately flew to my mother's face that day, and in just that moment, I felt his mind turning there as well, his laugh halting as he fell upon the deep well of missing that lives between us now.

There was nothing said for a moment, and I almost moved on into the kitchen. Then your gentle voice, as though you were considering your *nonno*'s pain but not responding to it, shared what your tone conveyed as a most personal detail. "My message was a true one," you said simply.

I heard a rustle then, which I took to be your *nonno* reaching for his handkerchief, and after a trumpeting blow, he asked, "What did it say?"

"It said, 'Live as you must and there will be much to live for,' " you replied.

I slid off then to complete my duties, but the conversation has stayed with me. Though it is not the one I meant to set down here, it does speak of your arrival and how you took to living in Rome with two people you barely knew. It speaks to your sensitive nature, and I walked away with the glorious image of you in a red tissue crown sitting at the wooden table in the cottage kitchen with candles glowing and a feast spread out around you. Which, if it is not exactly true, is likely quite close to it.

And so, you struck out on the journey to Rome on your own, in a carriage sent for you, and arrived with a glow on your face as though it was just as you had hoped.

I, on the other hand, was a bundle of nerves. I had not slept well for several days in advance—to the point where your *nonno* had given me a tonic to take the night prior to your arrival. Unfortunately, it had a paradoxical effect and left me wide-eyed and staring at the stucco ceiling as though I had consumed a full cup of *café au lait*! That is not the first time I have had an experience that runs in the face of the experiences of others, such as the remedy passed around in medical school that promised to keep you awake the full night that had me curled in the corner of the basement snoring loudly enough to wake the cadaver I was meant to dissect.

So, the day you were to arrive, I was quite wound up with lack of sleep and buzzing from the remaining effect of the tonic and no mother to settle my nerves. She would have surely taken me in hand and snapped me out of it, putting firm hands on my shoulders and catching my gaze as though to hypnotize. "Mimi, find your feet!" she would say with emphasis on the first and last word. And magically, at her command, I would land on my feet, anchored again in my body rather than swirling off in my head.

Remembering this, I was teary, but then I went to Papa and asked him to clasp his hands on my shoulders, and in full knowing, he parroted firmly, "Mimi, find your feet!" And then we both began laughing, which did, in the end, have the same result—to pull me from my unsteady head and looping heart back into my tired body.

Nevertheless, when the doorbell chimed, my startle response was that of a lesser vertebrate, and my body visibly jumped as though it were about to flee. That surprised Papa, and he looked at me with a mixture of concern and reprimand as he marched in a most determined manner to thrust open the front door.

From behind him, I could see you standing on the front step with a small bouquet of garden flowers in one hand and your valise in the other. I noticed immediately that it was unexpectedly elegant in brown leather, with a shiny clasp holding it closed. When your *nonno*'s eyes moved directly from your face to your case, I understood this had been his purchase as well. He had sent my favorite party snappers and a proper man's valise to my son, who was to come to live with us after fifteen years apart. This touched me so fully that with the lack of sleep and the nerves, I began to leak rather severely.

"Welcome home," your *nonno* told you, holding open his arms. You fell into them, and this was now too much for me to manage, and I stifled myself in my handkerchief, thrusting my full face into it so as not to cause a spectacle. That is when I felt your arms around me in your signature embrace—unquestioningly loving.

Your *nonno* had taken your case, and he was making a racket going on about the room that was waiting, and before I knew what was happening, there were flowers in my hand and he had taken you up the stairs and on into the next moment without me. For this I was very glad, and I suppose you both knew that. It allowed me some moments to collect myself and to put on the kettle for our tea.

By the time you had both returned downstairs, the tea was in the pot and a small repast was on the table, along with the flowers in a proper vessel. The two of you were in a back-and-forth about the journey and the sights you had seen on the way, and though the arrival had been emotional, it was jocular and full of spirit as well. We were all very glad to settle down at the table together to enjoy the meal I had created to welcome you.

Yet once we sat down, a not-knowing settled in unexpectedly. Though I had eaten countless meals around that very table, I felt like a stranger there with you. My heart began to pound with the not-knowing of it, and when I looked to your *nonno*'s face for reassurance, I saw a mirror of my own there. He shifted in his chair as though there was something itchy beneath him and adjusted his silverware without purpose, lifting it and placing it back down again.

You, who had never eaten at that table, seemed the most relaxed, though you looked at us to help you understand how meals began in the house. In an instant, my mother was with us, guiding what would happen next. That is the best explanation I can offer for what I did— that it was my mother coming through me. Sometimes when things go missing, we reach for them without knowing, and they are unexpectedly there.

Without thinking, I reached for your hand and your *nonno*'s and held them as my mother might have had she been there, causing your *nonno* to reach for your other hand so that we were all connected. This was what we did to mark special meals or special occasions—we held hands around the small table, and she offered some praise. So there we were - you in my mother's chair now - with linked hands, and there was nothing else for it but to complete the tradition. However, when I opened my mouth to speak, I found no sound would come out.

Both of you had instinctively bowed your heads when I took your hands, so there was no sight involved in knowing I had lost words, but Papa's voice filled in where mine might have been, as though that were the plan all along.

"Thank you for bringing Mario home to us today. Praise be to his arrival and to the days ahead." He ended as abruptly as he began, and offering a squeeze of the hand, he let us go. I looked to you to see how you had received this, wondering if he had squeezed only my hand or if it was to both of us at once. There was no indication either way, only that you looked pleased, and the moment had launched us into a passing and filling of plates, a pouring of steaming tea, a jot of cream, and then the slow and easy consumption of it all, with bits of replenishing and refilling along the way.

I have no memory of what we spoke about, though it was only a short time ago. Yet, perhaps more importantly, what remains with me is the happy way we shared that first meal, the smile that stayed on your face even as you were chewing, the laughs that burst out of each of us at one point or another. The small posy of flowers from the farm you brought had come back to life and was sitting prominently in the center between us, bringing a sense of wholesomeness, a sense of past into present, a sense of life into life.

Epilogue • 1875

Written by the hand of Maria Montessori's mother, Renilde Stoppani.

il 31 agosto 1875

What are the consequences of silence? There is a fury in my heart that will not abate even when night falls and another day has ended. Sleeping beside Alessandro and hearing the wind moving in and out of his solid body, which lies like a doorstop from the moment he arranges himself on the bed until the moment he rises. This used to soothe me, and now, in the five years since the arrival of Maria Tecla Artemisia, I find it perplexing that one can separate from the cares of the day so thoroughly and at will. This marriage is made real by the certainty that he will live a long life, likely longer than my own, as a result. And in the dark and quiet of the deep night, what is called into question is not his deep sleep, his peace, but rather my experience of the opposite. Before Mimi was born, I caged myself in convention, and it is her presence that now reveals that regularly. That I spend the days seeing through her eyes the conventions that surround us, noting my complicity.

So, the nights then are when the silence held all day is broken by the writing of these pages, the place where my words fall from the ink onto paper hidden in the kitchen drawer under the wrapped knives. Words so real that my hand shakes to write what is true after so much time of living only in my head.

Our daughter is magnificent. Her blaze is true and clear so that it can easily light Alessandro's fuse. The two of them are fire, and I watch them most days with great amusement. It does reflect back to me my own passivity, however, and I pray tonight, on her fifth birthday, that she does not waste the spice of herself to be lost in the giant vat of a man's important life.

il 29 settembre 1875

I have taken out these pages again, though it is another night at the kitchen table with Alessandro and Mimi asleep upstairs. It so rattled me to write the last sentence above that I was unable to sleep, and the next day found myself in one error following another, including dropping Mimi's morning egg on the floor as she handed it to me, her face glowing and alive.

Why does it unnerve me to see written on the page what I am often thinking? It is as though it gains power as the ink stains the leaf of paper. And the power builds around me so that I am leaking words to Mimi which have never before broken my lips—words of defiance, words of liberation. I half fear, half delight in the notion that I shall raise a rebel. Not an ordinary, docile woman who will fritter her ideas, her passions away, but one of boldness. May Maria be one of boldness.

il 8 ottobre 1875

Now I think that there is some potency in casting my thoughts to paper, for the morning following those last words, my child brought me a present she had made with her own hand. I held it, astonished that her work with a needle had become so capable, looking so closely at the stitches that I failed to notice the pattern on the fabric. I failed even to understand that it was a tea cozy measured to fit our pot precisely. Of this, I was so impressed that it was not until tucking her in that evening as I drew the curtains to a close that I realized she had taken the shears to them in order to sew my gift. I stood back, looking through the holes in the fabric to the darkening chicken yard, and I was speechless. "May Maria be one of boldness," I had declared. And it was so.

References

Kramer, Rita. *Maria Montessori: A Biography*, Monthly Review Press, New York, 1972

"Maria Montessori Biography." *Encyclopedia of World Biography*, 2006

Montessori, Maria. *Dr. Montessori's Own Handbook*. F. A. Stokes Co., New York, 1914

Montessori, Maria, and Carolina Montessori. *Maria Montessori Sails to America*. Montessori-Pierson, 2013

Moretti, Erica. *The Best Weapon for Peace: Maria Montessori, Education, and Children's Rights*. The University of Wisconsin Press, 2021

Standing, E. M, and Lee Havis. *Maria Montessori: Her Life and Work*. Plume, 1998

Acknowledgments

Though this book is fiction, it is based upon the work of other writers who sought to capture the life and work of Maria Montessori. Without their work, this book would not exist, and I'm grateful for the diligence they brought to the task of capturing that history. In addition, without the generosity of Montessori's family in releasing her diaries, this creation would lack dimension and depth.

Additional inspiration for the writing came from time with my own children, as well as time with the Boyle Literary Society on the farm in Maine. Many inspired prompts from the Emerging Writer's Group, as well as the Writer's Three group, made their way into here as seed ideas or fully realized pieces. I am grateful for the years they wrote alongside me, inspiring me with their own writing, as well as listening to mine.

In order to make its way into a final form, drafts of this book passed through the hands of some generous readers, including Pia Padukone, Toki Oshima and those in the Emerging Writer's Group. Final revisions were shaped by Tammy Letherer and Sarah Halper, who offered insights and feedback that pushed the manuscript to a better place. Without the dilgent copy-editing of Lynn Stevens, this hot-headed manuscript would simply be hot headed. I am most grateful for her deep knowledge of the

English language, the subject matter and the author.

Throughout the entire journey, Gedezou Sanon continued to meet with me regularly, offering encouragement, companionship, and support. This helped me to keep my momentum over the years. Thank you.

LAND ACKNOWLEDGMENT

This book came through me over years on the unceded land of the Agawam and the Nonotuck, two of many Indigenous groups from Kwinitekwa, the Connecticut River Valley, Massachusetts and also the unceded land of the Penobscot tribe of Abenaki people, overlooking the Penobscot Bay, in Maine. "The federal government's Indian Removal policies wrenched many Native peoples from our homelands. It separated us from our traditional knowledge and lifeways, the bones of our ancestors, our sustaining plants–but even this did not extinguish identity," writes Robin Wall Kimmerer in her extraordinary book *Braiding Sweetgrass*. I place this land acknowledgment here as a way to reconnect with our ancestors, honor the land we inhabit, and remind us to illuminate the identities of all those in our communities. I am grateful to the land and all that it has offered me, to the Indigenous people who cared for it, and in particular to the wise Venerable Dhyani Ywahoo, who continues to guide me, reminding me that we are all interconnected.

About the Author

ELIZABETH G. SLADE is the author of *Rest Stops*, a coming-of-age novel that won the Next Generation Indie Book Award in 2012. In 2021, she published the nonfiction book, *Montessori in Action: Building Resilient Schools* with John Wiley & Sons. Elizabeth has also worked with others to create books such as *Women Period.* and *How to Raise a Peaceful Child in a Violent World*. She is currently co-authoring *Finding Ground*, with Allison Jones, a book about teaching at the elementary level which is forthcoming from Parent Child Press.

In addition to writing, Elizabeth serves as the Executive Director of

Public Montessori in Action International, an organization committed to ensuring fully-implemented Montessori education for children, families, and educators of the global majority. Elizabeth earned her AMI Elementary Diploma from the Washington Montessori Institute, her AMS Administrative Credential at the Center for Contemporary Montessori Studies, and her Master of Fine Arts in writing from Spalding University.